SOMEONE ELSE'S STORY

PRAISE FOR
SOMEONE ELSE'S STORY

"States' characters are intense and finely crafted, their relationships are richly interwoven, and the terrors they endure and inflict are profoundly disturbing. *Someone Else's Story* unforgettably delivers heart and horror. Don't read it late at night. Trust me. You don't want it in your dreams."

– *Minister Faust*

"Laird Ryan States has mixed a midnight cocktail of pulpy occultism, international espionage, and gruesome delights. Drink it back in one heady gulp for best effect. Recommended."

– *Scott R. Jones*

ALSO BY
LAIRD RYAN STATES

FROM THE SEVENTH TERRACE

Sleeping Underwater
Sleeping Underwater – Souria Edition

Souria
Silver Bullets

THE SEL SOURIS CYCLE

Silver Bullets
Sleeping Underwater
Someone Else's Story

SOMEONE ELSE'S STORY

LAIRD RYAN STATES

Cover and Illustrations by
Janice Blaine

THE SEVENTH TERRACE

To Mary Shelley, and all the women who deal with the hubris of men who think they are gods.

To Gayleen Froese, who inspires me daily by being a better and more prolific writer than I am. Simple petty spite for this keeps my lazy ass writing. Also, you know, she's my best friend in the world and all of that.

To William Burroughs, who made me see exactly what's at the end of my fork.

To the people who gave their time in helping me refine my books, particularly Sky Sorenson and Katrina Maurer. They might like my writing considerably more than I do. I'm an ordinary man and as susceptible to flattery as a house cat.

Someone Else's Foreword

Based on our several decades of acquaintance, Mr. States is—and I think that I can say this without causing hurt—a delightful weirdo. His deep love for, and exasperation with, all of humanity are an integral part of him and I believe that exploring that has in fact made me a better person. His prose will immerse you in a delightfully weird world that reflects this understanding of what it is to be human.

Prepare to experience a setting that is almost—but not quite—the world that you already inhabit. It is, of course, weird. Perhaps Weird, if you want to discuss genre. It is completely believable and immersive however you describe it. The mundanity of the (W)weird for his protagonist Tom really helps cement the complete immersion in this alternate universe.

It's not just the setting that I am excited for you to read. Ryan writes characters who are dramatically different than I am, in important ways—and he has a talent for having me inhabit his protagonist completely. When I read his work, I feel Tom's romantic affections in a way that I don't while inhabiting my own self. That's a testament to how deeply he pulls his reader into the characters on the page.

Being completely immersed in a setting and character, unbroken by any Wilhelm scream type coasting, is a gift to the reader and would be enough for me to recommend the work. That's not all, though. All of that beauty is combined with turns of phrase that stop me in my tracks, setting down the work so that I can say to my self, "Well, if this isn't nice, I don't know what is."

I am distinctly excited that you're about to embark on the journey of the following pages. Enjoy, fellow reader.

- Sky Sorenson

A Note about Tom

I'm Laird Ryan States, and you'll see my name on the cover of this book as the author, but I'd say I'm more like a literary agent. Tom's pretending he's dead, and currently, as you'll read, living under an assumed name. This didn't keep him from fucking absolutely ripping me a new asshole when he wrote the foreword to the expanded hardcover of *Sleeping Underwater.* I guess that was important enough to tip his hand or something. I don't know. He's a new man when it's convenient for him, and mouthy as ever when he thinks he has something to say.

In any case, it's my turn to have a word about Tom.

I've known Tom for a number of years, now, and, when he lived close by, I would see him semi-regularly. He's an entertaining guy, always has a story on his lips, and a drink in his hand. I tend to be a sucker for older men who drink too much. Not romantically, as it happens, not that I'm his type. He likes twinks. I'm a bear. A big ol' bear at that. I mean as friends. I like to think I can save them, I guess. It's bad for me.

Anyway, Tom showed up in my life when I was starting to dream about Sel Souris, when some of my earliest online writing about it showed up. He was awfully interested and claimed to have had a lot to do with it. Naturally, I assumed he was an utter fucking crazy person, which, I mean, he is, but not in this particular.

When you practice magic, like I do, you sort of develop a flexible view of reality. To me, you see, Sel Souris is entirely a real place. Your mileage may vary. I've been there. I have family there. Most people, though, they just think it's ALL an arguably clever literary conceit. I'm okay with that. I'm not much for dogma.

Tom had a fuckton of stories. I ascribed to them the same objective reality that I ascribe to the spirits I summon and speak to, which is to say, none. I accept them as the truth when they are of value to me, and not when I have to deal with the mundane parts of my life like paying rent and doing the dishes.

I think that he found this irritating, and a little offensive. I'm not sure why. It's not like I wasn't listening. I helped him get *Silver Bullets* out in the world. We used my name. It was easier than the truth, and it's easier this time too. I'm getting his message out there.

When I took the massive patchwork of things he told me about his friends in England in the 80s, a lot of which he'd already gone on about in his book in the early 90s, *Sodomy and Gomrorrah,* and I decided to write a novelized retelling of it, I decided to publish it under my own name as *Sleeping Underwater.*

And frankly, why the fuck not? I listened to him tell this story piecemeal over the course of about ten years, with no structure or thrust. I put together, in my opinion, parts of the story he didn't seem to understand himself. I took this incredible mass of drunken, semi-coherent rambling, and I made it my own. He didn't write a word.

He's not even in that much of it.

I also reached out to Carter about it a little, and he was okay with it. His exact words, "Sure, it's not like anyone will believe any of it, and if it bothers Tom a little, that's funny."

I wrote it because I thought it was a beautiful story and it explained magic the way I've come to understand it. More beautiful questions than answers. I cared about those people. I didn't do it out of spite.

But lord, the offense he took, when he reached out after disappearing for just YEARS without so much as a call good-bye. He's lucky I took his call. A fella can get his feelings hurt when a collaborator and friend just ditch you.

He always told me he was indestructible, but I worried after his drunken ass.

In any case, he was so incredibly upset that he actually decked me, and after long negotiation, he wrote his over the top hostile foreword to the hard cover edition. He said a number of things about me that were unkind.

I'm not going to stoop to that any more than I have above. He is my friend, and despite all of the difficulties inherent in being friends with a surly drunk who chooses to vanish from your life for YEARS at a time, I cherish him.

That said, this book is just horse-shit. I would be hard pressed to say I believe as much as every other word. I think large parts of this book are designed to muddy the water about the history of Sel Souris, and how it recently sank. I think it's basically a propaganda piece, and it kind of pisses me off.

But here I am, his literary agent, and doing my job like a gentleman. He brings me the manuscript, and I publish it as is.

Did I show up at his apartment, throwing hands and demanding things? I did not. I am a civilized, fat, and lazy man, and he would have kicked my ass to the moon. Also, it would have been wrong.

Also, adding the particular rather famous character you'll find in the pages to come to the Sel Souris works is more than a dig at me. If it happened, the world is more insane than I dreamed. If it didn't, then fuck Tom.

I will say it's kind of entertaining. So, it's got that going for it, anyway.

-Laird Ryan States, Edmonton Canada, 2023

PROLOGUE

My name is Tom Bradstreet. I'm 62 years old, but look about 30. Long story. I'm five-foot-seven and weigh 135 pounds. My hair is light ashen blond. My eyes are blue. My back is covered with a series of lash scars I inherited from my father, a drunk who thought he was doing me a favour by toughening me up to face a harsh world. He'd be proud as hell of me now.

I'm currently in a shipping container, stowed in the storage decks of a freighter headed from British Columbia to Parts Unknown. It is pitch black in this container, and it has gone, over the course of the last sixteen days, from freezing cold to stifling hot.

It's not airtight, but pretty close. The air reeks from the five-gallon pail in the corner. I don't want to talk about that pail. I'm thirsty, and I'm hungry. I have, for supplies, eight saltines. Four cello-wrapped packets of two each. I haven't eaten any of them. I don't want to get thirsty. Thirstier. It's been fifteen days without water. I can put my finger inside my mouth and feel the skin of a lizard, dry and velvety. It's disturbing and I can't stop doing it. I pass my time by carefully walking back and forth. Six paces long if I'm careful and don't make my strides too big. It's hard to walk in total darkness, harder still because I'm dizzier than hell. I don't want to sit still because I'm afraid that I'll weaken further, that my legs will stiffen and I'll lose my chance to run the moment that door opens.

Fifteen days without water is a long time, twelve days longer than normal people would last. I got past the whole crazy pounding my fists bloody on the walls and screaming for water part of the adventure on the fifth day. Since then the thirst has retreated to a kind of silent alarm in the back of my head. I am never not aware of how badly I want water, but it's no longer all I can think of.

As I walk back and forth, I think of a lot of things, most of them not too clearly at this point. I remember growing up and getting larger. I remember moving away and going to school. I remember becoming a war journalist and traveling to exotic places, the sorts of places I used to read about in books and think of in the same way you might think of Narnia and Oz. I remember falling in love with two wonderful men, and fucking that up, and then a self- destructive period of sex and liquor and self-pity.

I remember the diagnosis, being told that my immune system was shutting down from the Gay Cancer, and that I'd almost certainly die in a few years.

I remember getting better.

I try not to remember how or why that happened. It should be easier, considering I only know half the story. I try not to remember what my life cost. I try not to see the mad, blind, mute man who died in a sick bed years after giving himself over like some kind of human sacrifice to die in my place. I try not to remember holding the pillow over his face, or the grey hair that surrounded it like a halo as he softly died. I remember everything, and understand nothing.

I think about how none of this might have happened if I carried a cell phone like a normal person. I'll look to that in future. Time has slipped away from me, and I'm resistant to change in so, so many ways. Sometimes I think that whatever happened to me has left me trapped forever in the eighties somehow. I'm a yellowing snapshot of a person in a digital world.

I decide to stop thinking. Instead I sing.

My voice sounds like a handful of machine parts rattling in an old tin can, and that's on a good day. Dehydrated, I find all that comes out is a croaking whisper, like the sound of two linen sheets sliding together. My lips are so cracked and dry that they split, and I taste my own blood as they try to form words.

I manage half a verse of Comfortably Numb before I give up, feel my way back to my usual spot and sit down again.

This voyage was not my idea. I suspect you'd sussed that out, but I want to spell it out. This is not a test or a stunt. I'm not on a reality show. I am not trying to push the limits, to see what it would take to actually kill me or something. I don't want to die, and I don't intend to spend time getting creative about seeing what may break me. Unfortunately, not everyone feels the same way.

The man who locked me in here calls himself William S. Frankenstein. I don't think that's his real name. He's already tortured me and ruined my life. Either he wants me to actually die in here, or he thinks he'll motivate me to share my magical secrets. He's going to be disappointed either way. I don't seem to be capable of death, and I don't know anything about magic at all.

Chapter 1: In Exile

Edmonton Alberta, 2010

Bradstreet, you've had enough," the bartender said, his huge hands, like overcooked slabs of steak, pressed flat to the bar. I looked up at him and smiled what I liked to think was a charming smile.

"Terry," I said, "I'm fine. I know I'm short and all, but I can hold my liquor like a champion. One more for the night, eh?"

His hands didn't lift off the bar. The towel he had over his left shoulder had slid halfway down the front of his "No Dead Chicks (fat chicks acceptable)" t-shirt, and only his heavy paunch kept gravity from claiming the prize. He had half a smile on his fleshy face; his full lips twitched slightly under his G. Gordon Liddy moustache.

"I know what you can and can't hold, man," Terry said, "You've been in here every night for a year now. I say you've had enough. In fact, give me your keys, asshole. I don't want you spreading yourself and some other guy all over the road."

I knew better than to argue with him any further, though my natural temperament pushed me hard in that direction. Terry was a huge man, and I'd seen him throw two men out of the place at once, one under either arm. I had no desire to lose what little was left of my dignity. I reached into my coat pocket and pulled out my key ring, setting it on the bar.

"There. Happy now, Christ."

He covered my keys with his hand. "Yep. Go home and sleep it off. You know how to find the place tomorrow."

I shifted myself off the barstool and straightened both jacket and hair. The room swum slightly side to side, and I closed my eyes until the world stopped moving. I opened them again, and Terry was dropping the keys in a large glass jar that once held pickled eggs. It had a jaggedly torn piece of paper scotch-taped to the side and the crude sign indicated the contents of the jar.

Keys for assholes.

It was about half full. The bar wasn't busy enough for this to be the proceeds of a single night's custom. I wondered what sort of man was so far gone he never came back for his car keys.

"Thanks, Terry," I said, feeling the shadow of the invisibly thin line distinguishing an alcoholic from a wino being cast on the back of my neck.

He nodded. "I'll see you tomorrow, Tom."

"To pick up my keys, surely. I may not drink."

He said nothing, bartender's discretion, and nodded again.

I headed out the front door, aiming for home. I should have flagged down a taxi, but I didn't live far. The night air was cool and brisk, and made me feel slightly sober and focused. Something nearby was burning. A good smell, but I felt a little ashamed at enjoying it. Probably someone's home, a whole life gone up at the whim of oxidation. Possibly insured, and possibly not, but you can never get back all the little snapshots of your pets and children, and all of the sentimental debris. I didn't have any of that, and I didn't like it.

I took a misstep, and my legs tangled. I stumbled forward and nearly fell over onto the parking lot of the instant loan and donair shops. The sudden lurch was answered by one in my guts, and I had to suck in a deep steadying breath not to leave a meal for the seagulls in the morning.

A car pulled up beside me, slowing. The passenger window rolled down. I was still not used to that being on the right. A lady poked her head out. She was made up for a night out, but her makeup had done the sort of drunken 3 a.m. slide you sometimes see, and it now looked gaudy and clownish, like a caricature.

"Fuckin' drunk!" she yelled, and the car sped up.

"Who are you to accuse me?" I shouted haughtily at the receding taillights, and I sounded ridiculous even to myself. "Christ."

I staggered the remaining half block to the intersection and crossed with the light. The motel neons and headlights were giving me a headache, and I wanted to throw up again in the worst way. I sat on a bench at a bus stop and put my head between my knees, breathing.

Pathetic.

It was light outside when I came back into something like awareness. My mouth tasted sour and dry, and I felt exactly as though I'd slept in my clothes on a public bench. I sat back up, gratified that I had not wet myself. The sun shone down on the deserted street. All the whores and drunks had staggered home except for me. I stood up and made my way back to the little apartment building in which I'd taken a basement flat. I closed the door, laid face down on my bed, and went back to sleep.

Now that I was halfway sober, the dreams came on full force. I was back in the old flat I shared with Carter and Victor, back when great lizards roamed the earth and sodomy was illegal on England's verdant soil. I closed the door behind me in the middle of the night. The two of them had curled together on the couch, with the telly still on. Carter curled up, small, handsome and owl-wise with his face pressed into Victor's neck. Victor's head lolled back on to the couch, and he snored lightly. The fan in the window tossed his shining ginger hair. I felt the same instant pain of total love and utter mystery that I always felt when I looked at them together.

I stepped closer and knelt down before them, not wanting to wake them up, just wanting instead to look at them a while with all their fortifications down. Beautiful and strange.

There was a ticking noise, and I looked at the floorboards. I saw nothing but, still on my hands and knees, I crawled to the baseboards, and laid my head down on the floor. I could see shapes in motion. The light changed in the room, shadows moving, and I looked back over my shoulder. A beetle crawled on the bare light bulb, showing no more concern for the heat than a salamander would.

I walked over, and looked up at it, purple and iridescent, and noticed that it was not alone. Dozens of them skittered across the ceiling and fell off to the floor, writhing and swarming at my feet. I should have panicked, but instead I just stared. None of them had been here a moment ago.

I looked back at Victor, and saw he was covered in them as well, and that they were crawling out of, but not into his mouth. Horrified, I drew closer and leaned over his face. From deep inside his throat came a deep and exotic scent of spice. His tongue was gone, cut off at the root and scarred lumpy, as it would be years later.

Suddenly, he opened his eyes, and the beetles crawled out and out over him and me and Carter and the whole room, and I felt them inside me, eating my disease and leaving something new and strange and cold and endless in its place. In the darkness I heard the clicking and chewing of a million beetles and saw the onrushing torrent of years beyond number.

The noise stopped then, and I was alone in the dark, pounding on the lid of a coffin, screaming myself hoarse. My screams echoed off the walls as though off of sheet metal.

I startled awake, soaked in sweat, and back in my flat. The afternoon sun came in through the little basement windows, and I heard traffic rolling by.

I made my way to the lav and took a long hot shower until my skin stopped crawling. I made toast and drank half a cup of cold, day-old coffee. I was not hung over. The dream clung to me like low fog and I realized I was waiting for it to disperse in the same way. I put the coffee cup in the sink, and the little plate as well, and went to check the mail. As I went into the hall, I saw my answering machine blinking. I cocked a head at it the way a dog might, and pressed the play button.

"Tom," the machine said, "this is Heather. I can't believe you are still in Canada. I can't believe you still use an answering machine. Are you ever coming home? Anyway, you should call me. I have a job for you, if you want it." There was a long pause. "I hope you're okay."

The machine beeped again and asked me if I wanted to erase the message or save it. I didn't know.

"Make an executive decision, machine," I said, and went out the front door.

Just up the stairs I stopped at the rows of mailboxes in what passed for the lobby and opened mine to find it empty of all but a couple of flyers. No royalty checks for Mr. Tom Bradstreet, but no bills either. A dead heat.

I remembered the way Victor's body had started to cool off so quickly, and how, even after just a few minutes I could feel the difference as I arranged his arms and his pillows to make it look as though he'd simply, finally, at long bloody last, gone in his sleep. I'd washed my blood from his lips and saw no spots on the sheets. Tears in my eyes, I'd stepped back into the hall and said goodbye to his mum and headed back for home. Whatever had happened to me to give me long life and make me so indestructible was not passed in my blood, or, if it was, it was just too late to help Victor.

A dead heat.

I slammed the little metal door shut, pressed the heels of my palms into my eyes, and shook my head.

"Oh Christ," I said, "Pull yourself together."

"Tough night, Tommy?" said Lisa, my upstairs neighbour, wearing a pair of ratty black jeans and a man's blue dress shirt. Her face was studded and ringed with a myriad of small bits of silver, as she was, apparently, afflicted with a mortal fear of werewolves or something. She was twenty, and a sculptor.

"Nah," I said, "just hung over. You know how it is, darlin'?"

"I don't drink," she said, ignoring the added Irish in my voice, as she was all too aware of my bullshit, "You might want to look at quitting yourself."

She sidled past me to open her own mailbox and pulled out a small armload of little pamphlets. She always seemed to be arm deep in them.

"Drink," I said, "makes long life bearable."

"And unlikely," she said, meeting my eyes with no fear at all.

I waved my hand in the air dismissively. "So, what are those bloody things, anyway?"

"Zines."

"Magazines?"

"Homemade magazines. They were mostly a thing when I was a little kid. They were like blogs before the internet ate our civilization."

"You're really very young to fear change."

She snorted and held a fist full of zines in my face. "These take some time to make, and to mail. People consider things. Twitter...that's instant social comment, and instant social humiliation. Forget it. Instant communication is going to make us all insane. Besides, who are you to poke me about being a Luddite? You don't even have a fucking phone."

"Well, there is some truth there, yeah. Still…" I squinted at the crudely lettered front cover; with its photocopied collage cover. "That doesn't look like high art either," I finished.

"Probably not. Most people have nothing to say," she said, and then winced. "No, that's elitist bullshit. They have stuff to say, they just don't have the skill to communicate it. Anyway, I'll trade zines with anybody. You never know."

"Well, whatever keeps you from robbing pensioners in the dead of night with the other delinquents, my dear."

"It's a hobby, you dick. It beats the hell out of drinking myself to death."

"I am not," I said haughtily, "drinking myself to death. I'm drinking to forget."

"Is it working?"

"I can't remember."

She rolled her eyes to the extent that you'd think we'd been married and took two steps up back towards her apartment.

"You want to see a movie later?" she asked me.

"Early show or late?"

"Early," she said. "I have a date later."

"Anyone you know?" I asked.

She gave me the finger and went on upstairs.

I laughed slightly, and realized she'd dropped one of her little zines on the ground. Without really thinking about it, I tucked it in my pocket, and walked to the bus stop to get downtown. I didn't have my car, and it would be several hours before Terry's place opened and I could get my keys. I decided to head to the library downtown and see if I could find a game of chess. Out of pure boredom, I fished the zine out of my pocket and looked at it. It was made from four sheets of folded 11x17 paper, and clearly handmade, done on a photocopier. The two staples were uneven. It was called *Verbally Transmitted Diseases*, and the front cover illustration looked as though someone had drawn an eight-legged goat with a crayon, and then ironed it into a long series of smears.

I turned the page and started to read it. It was fucking dreadful, but it passed the time.

Chapter 2: A Night at the Movies

"Heather," I said, "I'm calling you right now. I'm on the phone with you, Christ. Stop it."

"I called you two days ago. Where the bloody fuck have you been?"

"Love, I'm going to assume that your anger is a mask to hide your concern and your deep love for me. This should help us preserve our long friendship."

"Get stuffed, you cunt."

"Heather, for fuck's sake, I am calling you back. As you asked."

There was a moment of silence on her end of the phone

"Are you actually able to work right now?" she asked.

"I'm always ready to work."

"It would be easier for you to do that if you'd just move home."

"This is home now," I said, looking at the empty pizza boxes on my living room couch. "And you're a snob."

"I am not a snob," she said, sounding all the more toffee-nosed for it, "for thinking that you need to come back from the wilds of western Canada to civilization."

"That is exactly why you're a snob."

"Oh do shut up," she said, "you know what I mean."

"Do I?"

"Can you get to Vancouver for Friday?"

"I expect so."

"Right. Well, there's an exhibit opening there, on Friday. I need you to get an interview with the artist."

"They expecting me?"

"He's not taking our calls, actually."

I blinked a few times. "Really?"

"We've tried to arrange a phone interview with him several times."

"You're hoping that I'll have better luck face to face."

"It's your special gift."

I smiled. "So, what makes this guy worth your trouble?"

Heather didn't answer right away, and when she did answer her voice was a little troubled.

"Well, it's not his art, that's for certain."

Someone knocked on my door. "Heather, there's someone at the door. Just a tick."

"This is long distance and overseas, Tom. Hurry."

I set the phone down and went to the front door. I waved Lisa inside and headed back to the phone.

"Sorry Heather," I said, "It's the little neighbour girl selling cookies."

"Whatever. I will email you a package on everything and send you the e-ticket for your flight."

"Cheers. I'll email you back if I need anything."

"Tom?"

"Yeah?"

"There have been some stories. He likes to throw things. Through windows. So, if he says no, don't push it. Take no for an answer."

"I think I can handle it, dear."

"I know you do."

"Must run. Girl scout."

Lisa was sitting on my couch, with her feet up on the empty pizza boxes.

"I should have called first and given you a chance to tidy up. You must be really fuckin' embarrassed."

"Sorry," I said, "it is a little ripe in here."

"Dude," she said. "Dude."

She picked up a shoe from the couch and threw it at me. I batted it away.

"Can I help you out?" I said, and then sat at my computer chair, turning it on. It chimed as it started up.

"Well, we were going to do a movie so I thought I'd see if you had anything in mind."

"Sorry, Lise. I'd totally forgotten."

She extended her hand in some peculiar hand sign I didn't recognize. "Quel shocker."

I set down beside her on the couch and put a hand on her knee in an avuncular fashion. "I'll make it up to you. I'll pay."

"Good. So, what do you want to see?"

"I don't even know what's playing. You pick, and I'll be fine with that."

"K," she said, standing up. "Well as much fun as it is to sit here in your filth, I think I'll go do some work before then."

"Fair enough. I've got to fetch my keys from the bar anyhow."

"Classy. You're classy."

I bowed deeply from the waist, and as I stood up remembered I still had her charming little magazine.

"Oh right," I said. "You dropped something this morning." I fished it out of my coat pocket and handed it to her. "I read it. I hope that's okay."

"Any good?"

"It reads like it was written by the Son of Sam from his prison cell on Jupiter. The dog was his editor."

She smiled, and I felt the hard-won victory implied. She took it.

"Oh...oh yeah, this guy. He keeps sending me his zine, but I stopped sending him mine AGES ago. He is really special."

"It's a good thing his handwriting is so poor, or I might have understood certain parts of it."

"Guys like that that make me wish I had used a post office box, you know?"

"Yeah?"

"Yeah, but he lives in the States somewhere so I'm not too worried he'd just drop by."

"Well, that's all right then."

"Thanks anyhow," she said, and pushed her hair over her ear, which glittered with metal.

"See you tonight," I said. "Save room for popcorn."

"And one of those big ass candy bars."

"Fine by me," I said and closed the door behind her.

My computer was up and running and I checked my email. There was a message from Heather, with a bunch of links to various websites. I poured myself a glass of soda water and sat back down to get some preliminary research done.

The artist in question was named William S. Frankenstein. He had come to the attention of the art world for the first time with a show in Munich. A small affair at a small gallery of no particular reputation, but word of mouth spread quickly. He worked in mixed media. This was his term. In actual fact, he worked with corpses. He purchased human skeletons from Asia through grey market connections, and refleshed them with rotted meat from supermarkets and, it was said, animals purchased under the table from local pet crematoria.

He used these refleshed corpses in tableaus, some in imitation of famous paintings, and others in recreations of film sex scenes. His admirers said he was brilliant, his detractors called for his imprisonment. Certainly, he was closely watched by the various animal welfare societies. Not once could they prove any cruelty. It sounded wearying to me.

He did not do so well with the health boards. His Munich show was shut down after two days. The adjacent tenants complained of the smell that permeated the whole block. No number of fans seemed sufficient, and the conditions were by no means hygienic.

Frankenstein would not speak to the media, but did release a public statement, in English. It read, simply, "I'm sorry you didn't understand. Perhaps next time."

His next show had been in Chicago. He had enlisted two married terminal cancer patients to take part in a performance art piece. They displayed their lesions to the crowd, while a string quartet played a series of sixties rock pieces at half speed. At the climax of the show, the two patients began to make love with both tenderness and urgency. While they did this, entangled on the stage, Frankenstein came on stage, dressed in the robes of Death and carrying a scythe. He then used the scythe as a crude brush to paint images of the coupling on the large white backdrop in semi-congealed calf's blood. The sound of livestock being slaughtered faded in over the musicians, who eventually gave up altogether. The screams of dying animals became so loud that the audience (those who remained) began to demand they turn it down.

As if on command, his assistants began to walk up and down the aisles, offering what appeared to be actual firearms to any who wanted one. On each of the guns the words "Eat me" had been written in silver felt marker.

Frankenstein was arrested three hours later in his hotel room and out on bail by morning. Nothing ever came of the charges.

There was a lot more to read, but I took a break at that point. I walked around the flat a bit. I understood now, absolutely, why Heather was interested. What I did not understand, at all, was how I had not already heard of this guy. Those two performances alone were enough to get you some international attention, or so it seemed to me. That wasn't the case here. He had made a name for himself in certain circles, to be sure, but the mainstream media had passed on the stories. To me, that was almost more interesting.

He sounded like a real prince. On the other hand people freaked out about Alice Cooper and KISS too, and honestly there was more smoke than fire with both of those groups. I wondered how much of this had even happened, and how much was exaggeration by the pearl clutchers. I supposed I would find out.

The most interesting thing of all, though, more interesting than the works, or than the way his charges went away, was this media thing. I've met a lot of artists in my life. The one thing they had in common was that they wanted to be known. Most of them were complete whores for the slightest bit of attention. I could not fathom any artist, but especially a bloke going this far out of his way to shock, not wanting to talk to a reporter. It all seemed like a frantic cry for attention to me.

I sent Heather a quick email letting her know that I was going to get her an interview or wind up as part of his new show. She came back almost immediately telling me that I wasn't funny. Also, she sent my e-ticket.

I read through the rest of the stuff she'd sent me. A lot of samey-samey from that point, really. I was bloody certain Frankenstein was not his last name. I had no idea where he was even from. Nobody else seemed too either. It was as though he'd just shown up out of nowhere the night of his Munich show.

He certainly sounded German to me, but then I'm a bit of a bigot on that front.

I looked at the clock and saw that it was coming up on six, and I had a date with my protégé to think of. I shaved, washed up, and changed into something nice. I'd still forgotten to go and get my keys. This meant riding in her car, and her driving it. I decided to take a couple of Advil, just as a precaution.

Shortly thereafter, she knocked. I answered.

"Good evening, Lisa," I said. "You look lovely."

"Go fuck yourself," she said, her high breeding and charm school training evident.

She was dressed in another pair of black jeans, these untorn, and the same blouse as before. She had pulled he black hair back with a pale jade headband. She'd gone to some effort, and I hadn't been even slightly sarcastic. It was not in her nature or mine to do well with compliments.

"Oi, language," I said, pointing my finger at her. She blew a short raspberry at me.

"So," I said, "what are we seeing tonight?"

"It's called 'May'. It's playing at the Metro."

"A love story?" I asked, guessing better.

She laughed. "Yeah, it's a real chick flick."

I shrugged. "As you like, sweetheart."

"Where's your car?" she asked as we got outside.

"Still at the bar."

She looked at me. "So, we're taking mine?"

"It would seem."

She smiled broadly enough that I thought her earrings would snag on one of her lip rings.

I got into her car. It was a 1982 Toyota Tercel. It was absolutely clean inside. Her dashboard wasn't even dusty. There's a difference between tidy and ill, and she had crossed that line in this car. The car smelled of cinnamon and apples, or one of those air fresheners that claim to.

She reached above her head to grab a pair of fingerless driving gloves from between roof and visor. She put them on, her long black fingernails still on full display, just in case anyone forgot that she was a dweller in darkness, and that no mortal would ever understand her. She pulled a cassette from a case between the front seats and slammed it in the tape player. I braced for it.

She shifted the car into drive, enjoying my discomfort. Noise came from the speakers, like two skinned cats fighting in a large pickle jar. At a volume that actually made my bones hurt, and she frantically bobbed her head to the machine gun rhythm.

I could say nothing, for we had long since established that the driver picks the music. Even if I tried to say something, I would not have been heard. I just forced a smile, grabbed the little handle on the ceiling to my right, and tried not to notice that she was driving twice the speed limit with the caution of a meth addict. She said something I could not, in my wildest dreams, have made out over the din. I nodded vigorously.

We pulled into the underground parkade for the Citadel Theatre and she stopped the noise. For a second, my ears rung.

"You know," I said, "in an email to my boss I referred to you as my protégé. That was the wrong word."

"Next time, go with caregiver."

"Cheeky bitch."

We got out of the car and headed to the stairs. It's a half flight that leads into the Citadel's conservatory, a lovely indoor forest of small size. Emerging from the parking lot always felt a bit like ending up in Oz. Lisa smiled and breathed deep.

"It's warm here," she said, and sat on one of the benches. "We have a few minutes."

I sat down beside her, and we didn't have any need to talk at all. Some little birds twittered above us, and music drifted from some concert in one of the auditoriums.

"Well," I said, quoting Kurt Vonnegut, "If this isn't nice, then I don't know what is."

"You said it, Papa Kurt," she said.

I'd met Lisa the morning after Kurt Vonnegut died. I'd been in the building for two weeks then. She was sitting on the stairs, with her face in her hands, still holding the newspaper where she'd read it. I asked her what was wrong, and she told me, and I joined her in weeping, the two of us leaning against each other and just bawling like babies. Irish men have no issue with tears. She was the one who felt embarrassed. It's hard not to be friends with someone after that.

She reached over on the bench and gave my hand a little squeeze before she stood up. "Come on Grandpa," she said. "It's time to see the chick flick."

I slapped her ass with a completely chaste smirk and she kicked me in the shins with her black skinhead boot. "Hey now," I said.

"You slapped my ASS!"

"You called me Grandpa."

"Well, so what if I did. You're sixty-two. Get used to it."

I swallowed a little. It's not like anybody was going to believe her. On some level, I don't think she actually believed it, but it made me nervous to speak of it in public. The Metro Theatre was just one of many auditoriums at the Citadel, but unique in that, while the rest were for live theater, it was for showing films. It was on the main floor, steps from the conservatory.

"Ixnay toots," I said, from the corner of my mouth like a gangster from an old movie, and we walked up to the ticket seller.

He was a kid in his twenties, long brown ponytail and glasses, a volunteer, god love him. I asked for two tickets.

"This is my friend, Tom Bradstreet," she said to him. "He's sixty-two years old, was born in Belfast, and is going to live forever."

The ticket taker smiled. "That's nothing. I'm Connor McLeod of the Clan McLeod. I was born in 1518 in the village of Glenfinnan on the shores of Loch Shiel and I cannot die." He mimed stabbing himself.

"Oh my god," Lisa said, "that is so hot."

She leaned over the counter jokingly trying to kiss him.

"Sixty percent of the time," he said, "It works every time."

We laughed and went to the snack counter.

"Hey," she said, frowning. "I saved room for the big chocolate bar! No fair."

"When you picked the venue," I said, "you knew they only have the small ones here."

"Stupid logic," she said, and ordered two of them, and a popcorn.

We settled into our usual seats three rows from the front. That's too damned close at most theatres, but not at the Metro.

"You know," I said, "My condition is meant to be a secret, right?"

"Pshaw," she said, pronouncing it as a word, with a hard p no less. "You just saw the reaction."

I wasn't going to win the argument, and so I just let loose a long-suffering sigh, as she munched contentedly on her popcorn. The lights went down and the movie came on.

It was not a chick flick. It was a story about a crazy loner lady who builds a perfect lover for herself out of some dead bodies and other things she keeps around the house. The coincidence inherent in this did not give me pleasure. I don't enjoy coincidences at all. I think they are the world's way of trying desperately to get your attention.

She liked the film considerably better than I did, giggling still as we left. We paused again in the conservatory, and I looked at my watch.

"When do you have to be home?" I asked.

"Oh, a couple of hours. He doesn't get off work until eleven."

"Which he is it this time?" I said, trying not to sound exactly the way that I did, in fact, sound.

"It's the one you like," she said, rolling her eyes.

"I don't like any of them."

"Aw. That's sweet."

"No, sincerely," I said, "I haven't liked any of them."

"That's funny. I'm pretty sure you've checked out at least one or two of their asses."

I laughed. "Christ. That doesn't mean I like them or approve of them. It just means they might be a little pretty."

"Well, Tommy, just at this point in my life, all I'm looking for is a little pretty for a couple of hours."

"Spare me all talk of anyone tampering with your delicate nethers. I was going to offer to buy us a quick snack."

"Snack!" she said, hopping in place and clapping her hands. "Snack!"

"I thought so. Christ, when your metabolism slows, you're going to turn spheroid."

She ignored me and we walked to the car.

"Hey," I asked, "have you ever heard of William S. Frankenstein?"

Lisa stopped walking suddenly.

I stopped too, and looked at her. She looked like I'd just asked her to go down on me at her Gran's 85th birthday.

"Lise?" I asked, putting a hand on her shoulder, and she stiffened and then started walking. "Shit," she said, trying to sound detached and light, but her voice had a quaver in it. "I forgot. He's getting off early, and I'm supposed to pick him up. Can you make your own way home?"

"Sure. I... Is everything okay, pet?"

"Sure. It's fine. I'm sorry. Thanks for the movie. I need to go."

She pulled away leaving me there in parking lot alone, not sure what just happened. She was a moody one, my Lisa, and sometimes she just went off. I didn't always know why, and I never pressed. It always blew over in a day or two. The world is complicated and we're all a bunch of wrecks.

I walked back up the steps into the soft warm green and stayed there for a while, my eyes closed, remembering tropical places and the sound of gunfire in the distance that seemed to walk hand in hand in all of my memories.

I went out into the chilly fall air and pulled my black leather jacket tight around me. It was older than Lisa, and had been with me every place I had ever gone. It made me feel safe and, if not warm, at least comforted.

It seems she'd heard of William S. Frankenstein. Where had I been?

Terry's bar sat next to a quite out of place pastry shop just off the main road. I paid my cab and went to my car. No graffiti, no stolen hubcaps, and no broken glass. I was moderately pleased as I went inside and sat at the bar, on my regular stool.

"Evening, Terry," I said. "How's your night, mate?"

"Quiet. I'd have thought I'd seen you by now."

"I had a date with a lovely young lady."

"Must have gone well," he said, looking at his watch.

I smiled. "It seems I said something impolite."

"No nooky for you, then, eh?"

"I'm queer anyhow, so it's for the best."

"That little weirdo lives upstairs from you?"

"Oi, she's my friend, Terry."

"Still a weirdo. She looks like the Bride of Frankenstein."

My stomach quivered. "At least she isn't boring."

"I hear that," Terry said, smiling. "What's your pleasure tonight?"

"A week in 1979," I said, "but barring that, I'll have a Guinness, Christ."

He didn't have Guinness on tap, but he had begun to stock a supply of it in the cans since I'd become a regular. He pulled one, warm from its carton, like a good man.

"Just one, tonight, Terry," I said, "Then I've got to get home. I've got to make arrangements to leave town for a few days."

He turned, and poured it into a glass for me with steady hands that had clearly poured a million drinks. His face was focused but relaxed. Every once in a while I am able to see and truly appreciate the craft and skill in everyday work. He set the beer down on a paper coaster in front of me, and I felt a little bit like applauding.

"You're an artist, sir," I said, appreciating the head and lifting it to my lips.

For a moment I just sat and listened to the dim mumbling of the jukebox, and looked at the Hockey highlights on the silent screen in the corner. I suspect I will never understand how the game works, but it's pretty to watch with all the whizzing around back and forth on skates.

Once I finished the beer, I nearly asked for another. My hindbrain screamed for one, in fact. I put my hands on the dark scarred wood and stood up.

"Jesus," Terry said, "you were serious? You've been saying 'just one' for months."

"I have an assignment."

"What do you do, anyway?"

"Freelance journalist."

"Huh," Terry said, setting his rag on the bar. "I did not know that."

"What did you think I was, then?"

"I dunno. Not that, though."

"Keys, if you please?"

Terry handed me the jar and I found my keys very quickly. "Where are you headed?"

"Vancouver. Just gone a couple of days and then I'll be back here drinking."

Terry nodded. "Don't take this the wrong way, Bradstreet, but there's no law saying you have to."

I smiled, my eyes feeling just slightly hot. "Just my nature, mate. I'm a wretched failure. This is where I belong."

"Nice," Terry said, bristling a little.

"Well, don't take it the wrong way," I said, with a little smirk.

He tossed his rag at me and I left with it over my shoulder to preserve the dignity of my exit. I was halfway home before I realized I might have actually had an impact on the functioning of his business. From the smell of it, he had used the rag for about a million years without washing it. Maybe he didn't have another.

I turned on the telly to the CBC. *Ghost of Frankenstein.* I turned it off immediately, went to bed and lay there most of the night staring at the stucco on the ceiling.

Chapter 3: Fragility

I waited at the mailboxes for a while, hoping Lisa would stop by. After sitting on the stairs for several minutes examining junk mail and enjoying the slightly musty ambience and grotty yellow brown industrial carpeting, I gave up, walked to the back door and looked for any cars I didn't recognize before doing the same in the front. I was then reasonably sure that, if she were at home, she was there alone. I didn't want to knock and deal with all of that awkwardness.

I steeled myself outside her door and knocked.

I heard the sound of shuffling and rustling, and bare feet stomping to the door.

"Who is it?" she said, slurring it all into one angry word.

"Tom Bradstreet, gentleman plumber. I hear you got a problem with your pipes," I said, in my worst Hollywood porno accent. I sounded like Keanu Reeves doing an impersonation of an Irish Tom Waits. It was very bad.

I thought I heard a snicker from inside.

She unlocked the door and looked up at me sheepishly. She was still wearing her clothes from last night, and I could see her boots lying in the hallway, where they'd been kicked. Her apartment smelled, as always, of paint and Chinese food.

"Hi Tom," she said softly.

"Just wanted to see that you were all right?"

"Yeah, I..." she sighed, and said, "I'm okay. I'm sorry. You wanna come in?"

"Sure," I said and closed the door behind me. Her place was not as neat as her car, but it was certainly well organized. Her problem was the classic problem; she had too many things for a place she could afford. Her canvases were rolled up and tucked into every available crevice. She had her easel on a drop cloth in the middle of her living room. She had been working on something for the last few days. She did abstract stuff, and I didn't pretend to understand it, but I'd long since given up mocking it. Either the Emperor is naked, or everyone else knows something you don't. In either case, you'd best stay quiet if you want any human contact that means anything.

She pointed at the coffee maker. "Have some if you like."

"I'm fine, thanks. How was your date?"

She glared at me, as though I'd said something stupid again, and perhaps I even did. Then she looked at the floor, ashamed. "Didn't go," she said.

I sighed and leaned against the wall looking at her. "I'm sorry I upset you last night, love. Honestly, I didn't know that was a sore spot."

"How could you? Don't be stupid," she said, interrupting forcefully, "I'm just being a psycho like usual. Bleh."

I shrugged. "We've all got our little zones of psychosis. It's fine, honestly."

"What do you want to know about Frankenstein for?"

"That job I was talking to my boss about. They want me to go to Vancouver and interview him for the Sunday."

Her jaw dropped open and she stared at me goggle-eyed.

"Why does everyone in the world seem to know about this person except me?"

"I don't know, Tommy. No offense but sometimes it's like you don't seem to know about anything that didn't happen like fifty years ago."

"Great. Are you going to say anything else or just stare at me with your mouth open, Christ?" I winced inside as I said it. She closed her jaw with an audible click, well heard above the awkward silence.

"What do you want to know?" she said, with a cold edge to her voice.

"Nothing, if it's going to make you angry."

"I'm not fucking angry," she said, pointing her finger at me, "and if you spent more time paying attention to other people instead of drinking, you'd be able to tell the difference."

I raised my hands as if to ward off blows and took a step backward.

"Okay," I said, "fucking hell! I feel like I'm juggling hand grenades. Christ."

"I'm scared!" she said. "Asshole."

"You may be just a little angry, as well," I suggested.

"You're winning that argument."

"Lisa, for the love of God and all his brothers, if you don't want to talk about it we don't have to. Just tell me what you want."

She looked at her knees for a moment. "It was just you bringing him up right after that movie. It was creepy coincidental, you know. I felt like I was being watched by something in the corner that wanted to eat me, and that you were just, I don't know, some kind of stick puppet it was using to lure me in."

"I understand," I said.

"Get out," she said. "You do not."

"I do so. I was reading about him before we left, and thinking about what his message might be, if he has one, and then you walk me into that little number of a film, and it felt like well, as you say, creepy coincidental."

She stood up and threw her arms around me, and I hugged her back.

"I love you, Tom," she said.

"You too, kid."

She pulled back and turned from me so I wouldn't see if she'd misted up. She hated being a girly-girl.

"Was that all it was?" I asked, and she shook her head side to side.

"No," she said, pointing to the coffee table, and a DVD with a handwritten label. "A friend of mine in Montreal sent me that a month ago. It's totally underground, passed hand to hand."

"What is it, exactly?"

"It's a short film Frankenstein made. Marcel told me that it made the *Guinea Pig* films look like *Cannonball Run*."

"What's *Guinea Pig*?"

"It's a series of ultra-gory horror films from Japan. The first couple were pretending to be real snuff films, and then from there they started to develop plots and stuff. The first two fooled a couple people, and there was a big controversy until more people actually saw them. I mean, they're gross and everything, but you don't need a medical degree to tell it isn't real. Mostly they are just psychologically icky, you know? Like you want to wash your eyes after."

"I feel like that after half the movies you show me, and I spent four months in Liberia in the late eighties."

"Well, Marcel was right. I didn't talk to you about it. I didn't talk to anybody about it. I wanted to throw it out, but I couldn't believe what I had. I didn't sleep for days, and I'm still having bad dreams. When you came out with that out of the blue like that, it felt like I was in the middle of a bad dream all of a sudden."

I nodded. "I completely understand. Believe me. Can I watch it?"

"You can if you want, buddy, but not in here. If you want my opinion, I'd say don't. I think that movie is like the videotape in *The Ring*. People who watch it are fucked up forever."

"Forever's a long time. You seem okay to me."

She shrugged. "I'm sorry I freaked out last night, for real."

"Forget it."

She looked me in the eyes and she looked so young that it made my heart ache. She had so much before her, decades and decades and decades and was still not tired of it. I slipped the disc into my coat pocket.

"Tom," she said, "I know it's your job, but I don't think you should go. I think he's a monster. A for real monster like out of a story."

"So am I."

"You're not. You're just a normal person except for that one thing."

"It's a pretty bloody large thing."

"Not to me," she said, "to me it's just cool."

I smiled. "Well, you can relax. It's not as if he can kill me."

She shuddered and answered quietly. "I know that, Tom."

I didn't understand how far ahead of me she was until after about ten days in the container. I just smiled and put a hand on the side of her face.

"Stiff upper lip and all that. I'll be back before you know it, and hopefully I'll have put a hole in his image big enough to put him out of the public mind for a while."

She smiled weakly. "Okay."

"Okay."

The click of her door behind me sounded unusually final and bleak. I went downstairs to my place and cracked a beer to watch the DVD.

A hazy burst of electronic static before the screen went dark. Lines and faint roll on the signal indicated this had originally been shot on videotape. The credits were old school Video Toaster, with the blue lines and some noise as the film announced its title, "Fragility."

The darkness seemed to fade from the screen and to a pure white. After a moment I realized that I was looking at porcelain. I could tell this from the reflection of the light. Just as I realized that, the pristine white surface was spattered with a fine spray of dark red.

Someone breathed in sharply just as one sometimes does when they've done themselves an injury.

The screen faded to black again, and the words "A William S. Frankenstein Film" jittered on the screen.

Jump cut to what looked like a medical laboratory, with an examination table. When you looked closer, though, you could see that it was really just the table. The rest of the room was a well-done series of paintings on heavy canvas curtains, which had been stretched taut. For a second you believed the illusion, and then it burst like a bubble.

A voice over began. "My name is William S. Frankenstein, and this is where I was born."

Jump cut to a woman on her back, her skin pale and cold. We pull back and see that she is on the table. A doctor walks into frame and speaks into the microphone hanging over the body.

"The deceased is a woman, Caucasian. She is 5 foot 7, appears to be in her mid-thirties, in an advanced state of pregnancy. There are no visible signs of injury, no bruises or contusions. There are a number of old scars across her chest, long healed. Subject was likely the victim of childhood abuse. Subject died on arrival at hospital, seemingly from complications in delivery. I am preparing to make the first incision."

The actor sounded like he was reading his lines, his voice weak and slightly lispy. So far, this felt like a student film, and not a good one. The woman, on the other hand, was playing an admirable corpse.

The "coroner" ran his scalpel from between the woman's breasts and over her belly. Suddenly, the belly twitched visibly, and the doctor stepped back, dropping the scalpel.

"Dear God," he said, and he stumbled out of frame to the telephone. He called for assistance as the belly shook and quivered. The camera moved in closer, into the dark of the opening wound.

Another jump cut, almost comic, to several bloody doctors standing around the table, and the sound of cutting. Blood sprayed up over them, and a laugh track blared as they pulled something free and held up a baby. My breath caught in my throat. Its head was misshapen, and lumpy, one eye bulged out and the other sunken in. One arm was twice as long as the other. It squirmed in the hands of the man who held it, opening and shutting its mouth in a desperate struggle to scream. When the noise finally came, all the men cheered.

The screen faded to black.

I heard footsteps and a faint feminine whimper. The lights came up and a man stood in front of the table, backlit to reveal only his shape. He was tall, monstrously so. One of his shoes had a thick platform to even up his legs. One of his arms was longer than the other.

"My name is William S. Frankenstein, and this is where I was born, crawling my way out of bloody flesh like anyone else."

He pulled a knife from his cloak, glinting as he slashed it across his other forearm. The blood spattered against the floor, and he breathed in sharply. The sound from the opening shot.

"My name is William S. Frankenstein, and today I am getting a divorce."

Two men in masks pushed their way into the light, setting the whole painted set to wobbling. They dragged with them a woman with long dark hair and hollow eyes. Her face was a mask of old healing cuts, and they tied her to the table. Her screams were terrified. She was a good actor, or this was for real. She was a good actor.

Frankenstein turned his back to the camera sparing me the sight of his face. The knife, still bloody, plunged into the woman. Blood spurted and she screamed. When she did, a bubble of blood formed and burst on her lips. He stabbed and slashed over and over. My skin went cold. I did not believe, could not believe, that this was make-believe. I saw the moment the life left her eyes. The camera zoomed in for it, for the moment when the subject became an object, and somehow he caught that on film.

The camera lingered on those dead eyes and did not flinch. All that could be heard was heavy breathing.

The film rolled backwards at high speed and then stopped a few frames before the light went out. Back and forth, the footage went. Alive, in agony, then dead, then alive, then dead. I felt like I was watching an analysis of the Zapruder footage.

The voice over continued, "It's not a long show, but it is fascinating. The rest of it takes days."

Frankenstein took a pair of handcuffs and fastened one end around his wrist, and the other around the woman on the table. The camera moved overhead, the same perspective as the autopsy scene.

He whispered something to the corpse, and soft string music faded up. Time-lapse photography started. I saw its eyes sink in, its belly swell. After a minute the insects started in. All the while, Frankenstein was there, growing slightly thinner. There was a bucket near his feet. The flies swarmed it too. The body came apart over the course of a long half hour. Then time snapped into normal speed, and he simply walked away from the corpse. The end of the cuff on its wrist had room to come free of the wet bones writhing with slime and dead maggots, but it jerked the corpse to the floor.

I will remember the sound as it landed for as long as I live.

The screen went black, and I heard, "I, William, take you, Miranda, to be my lawful wedded wife for better and for worse, in sickness and in health, until death do us part."

The chroma key letters came on the screen at the same time as Frankenstein's voice over. "Born again, I've never loved her more."

The sentence glowed on the screen for a moment longer and the screen went dark. That wasn't an art film, it was a psychotic episode, and, I believed in my guts, the real thing.

The Internet, however, said I was wrong. According to the Internet, William S. Frankenstein was still married to a Miranda Efrit, who took part in his exhibits regularly. There were photos of her taken five years after the film.

And still I believed the film, which either made it excellent or terrible.

CHAPTER 4: TO ABSENT FRIENDS

Heather called me at my hotel in Vancouver, to my surprise. I had just laid down on the bed and kicked my shoes onto the floor. I'm not a good flier, and I was doing my best to unwind. The flight had been especially unpleasant. There was something wrong with the ventilation system and there was a loud rattle that, while it had no consequence to the operation of the vehicle, was not anything I wanted to listen to while floating above the mountains for an hour.

"Have you settled in, then?" she asked.

"Just starting to, yeah."

"Something wrong?"

I closed my eyes. "Not really. I've been doing my due diligence on this cunt. It's ugly work."

"Saw *Fragility*, did you?"

"Yeah."

She didn't say anything for a second, and line was silent. I remembered only ten years back when there was always hum in an overseas call. No longer.

"Nice bit of work isn't it?" she said, sounding less thrilled even than you'd expect.

"Yes," I said, "it certainly isn't."

"Well," she said, "use caution."

"The hell with that," I said. "I hate this guy, and I intend to do a hatchet job on him that will make Frost/Nixon look like a tea party."

"That's a very poor attitude for a professional journalist to have, Tom," she said with a smile in her voice.

"I am chastened. The trick, of course, is to make him look like an arse without seeming like some little old lady in a church committee."

"Perhaps you'll make him cry," she suggested.

"That would be a get."

"Miss you, Tom. Come home soon."

"Home isn't home anymore, Heather. Miss you too."

We hung up, and I took a brief nap. My dreams were not pretty. Mostly they were of Victor. Some of them were of the sound of the Bride of Frankenstein hitting the floor.

When I woke up I was not alone. A man in a suit occupied the chair beside my bed, smoking a cigarette, and looking out the window.

"Hope I didn't wake you," he said.

"No. Thanks."

I clenched a fist where he couldn't see it, shielded behind my body. "I'm sorry about the cigarette," he said. "I got edgy waiting."

I had no idea who this was, but his voice was British. He seemed to know me.

"Not a problem, mate. Who the fuck are you?"

"Oh, right. So sorry," he said, looking embarrassed. "It's me, Cathy, from the Sideshow."

I exhaled with some relief. "Jesus, Cath. You ought to wear a bloody sign."

She laughed with this stranger's voice. "Sometimes I forget. I jump around so much these days."

"You picked the wrong damned day to sneak up on me is all. I'm awfully bloody worked up. Christ."

"I'll just bet you are. I have a sort of assignment for you, Tom."

"I'm a civilian now."

"Oh please. Nobody leaves the Sideshow. MI-13 is a lifetime appointment."

I started to pace, and I wanted one of her cigarettes, but I promised myself I wouldn't pick up that filthy habit again. I wasn't filled with dread anymore, I was as angry as hell.

"Listen to me, Cathy, and listen well. I will not do dirty work for Her Majesty's Mystical Monsters ever again."

She rolled her eyes and looked absolutely like the little woman I remembered from years before, despite the well-kept rugged good looks of her current victim.

"You make it sound like we had you shooting Soviet moles. All you ever did for us was talk to people that might have killed someone less durable. Better you than someone else, after all, and better, I would think than us just killing them outright without trying to change their behaviour."

"What the hell do you want?" I asked.

"I want you to convince Frankenstein to stop doing art, and seeking attention, and to just go back to being a terrible monster in the dark."

"Go to hell," I said. "You're, all of you, as bad as he is."

"Someone has to police the freaks, Tom."

"No, they bloody don't."

She sighed, and put her cigarette out in the ashtray. "Do what you like. You will anyway. But do us all a favour and ask him about the Al-Asad fragment. See what happens."

"What's that?"

"Ask him, seeing as you're such a clever little bastard. It would serve you right if I left right now so you could explain to this gentleman why he's in your room. You're lucky some of us have a sense of responsibility where our talents are concerned."

"Oh for fuck's sake, that is a desperate flail even by your standards. Get out."

Cath slammed the door behind her, and I immediately felt like rubbish. She wouldn't have barged into my room unless it was actually important. MI-13 had, I supposed, been good to me, but I couldn't get past the notion of working for the English, and I couldn't trust their motives. Not ever. Mostly I felt like rubbish because it was simple revulsion. I didn't like them because they were a pack of freaks, just like me. Each with their own little quirks, and each trained to be a little attack dog for Big Brother.

The rest of us out in the night were only able to live our weird lives insofar as the Sideshow let us. They were the magic police. By necessity, they were a secret police. I couldn't stomach that, either. I'd had enough Gestapo tactics under Thatcher for a lifetime.

On the other hand, what other options were there? And I knew the good they'd done for me, and for Carter and for Victor in helping me to quiet down all the nasty business surrounding what had happened to him.

It renewed my appreciation for drinking and watching movies with the neighbour girl, and ignoring the world entirely.

I needed the money, and worse still, I was curious. I couldn't walk away.

Part of me wanted to do just that, and very badly. I wanted to crawl back to my flat, and apologize to Lisa for bringing Frankenstein into our little lives and go back to being layabouts. Of course, Frankenstein had already hurt her. That was in some ways the thing that was the biggest spur. He'd made her feel dirty, and I wanted to kick his teeth in for him. Macho bullshit is a bitch, and I'm unfortunately fucking swimming in it.

Now Cathy, acting as the voice of authority, had confirmed my worst suspicions. Frankenstein was more than a nasty human weirdo, he was One Of The Bad Monsters. Because I am a prideful prick, I'd kicked her out before she could give me any useful information.

87

Chapter 5: On the Town

I took a cab to the gallery, a tiny place a block off Commercial Street. It was raining as I went inside. Everyone gathered in a small anteroom, and most were dressed formally. A small group, mostly local artistes, and the university crowd. I felt slightly out of place in a black leather jacket and slacks, but it's okay to stick out slightly as a journalist.

A black drape with a red velvet rope in front kept the show a secret. There was also a cash bar. Nearly everyone carried a drink. I looked for familiar faces and saw none. I had my digital recorder in my pocket, and a large knife in a hidden sheath at the small of my back, under my jacket. The weight of both were very distracting.

By the standards of most of the galleries I had been to, though, it was a little drab and second rate, and so were the people in attendance. Vancouver is a world-class city, but this wasn't up to standard. It wasn't even up to the neighbourhood standard. It was grasping, too small, which made it feel even more crowded.

A sudden murmur went through the crowd, and I saw her for the first time. It was Miranda Efrit, the woman I'd watched decompose. She was looking much better now. Her eyes were rimmed with kohl, and her long hair plaited in a faux-Egyptian style. Her facial scars were highlighted with blush. Her tight, nearly transparent dress swept along the floor. She whispered to a small balding man in shabby suit. Then she'd slunk back through the side door again.

A moment later, the small man unlatched the rope, pulled back the drapes, and we wandered inside. I did not know what to expect, but I'd prepared for the worst. I took a last deep breath before I plunged in. What I saw left me puzzled and a bit...well, disappointed isn't the word. It was not what I expected, let's say.

It was a series of treated photographs. Black and white landscapes, mostly. On these landscapes he had superimposed images of antique Ferris wheels. The lighting was harsh and there was something sinister in the banality of the images and the constant repetition of the Ferris wheel, but honestly, it only seemed sinister in light of his previous work. If the exhibit had been the work of a middle-aged housewife named Betty Graham, it would have seemed very normal.

The looks on the faces around me ranged from relief to shock to anger. One man angrily shouting that this was some kind of a joke and was escorted out by two staff members. Over twenty minutes passed, and Frankenstein did not make an appearance. His wife, on the other hand, watched closely from the corner. Nobody approached her. Some wandered in her direction, but then veered away as if gently nudged.

I walked up to her. "Ms. Efrit," I said, "I'm Tom Bradstreet with the *Guardian*. Is William here tonight?"

She looked at me as though I had splattered on her windshield. "Why would he bother?"

"It's customary for an artist to attend the opening of his exhibit," I said, "Is there something that's made him unhappy about it?"

She smiled. "Nothing in particular. I think we can all agree it's not his most personal work."

She offered me a hand to shake, and I took it. The moment her skin touched mine I smelled death on her. Violets and formaldehyde. I felt the knife plunge into her and felt that she liked it. She looked into my eyes, and knew that I knew. Her smile was cold. She knew I was shaken.

"Run away now, little reporter. You amuse me, but William will not speak with you. He doesn't do what he does for fame. Neither do I."

I smiled, and let go of her hand, feeling an intense relief at the end of whatever invasion she'd subjected me to. I laughed politely.

"No offence, but I'd rather hear it from William. I mean, I've come a long way. If this is all there is to the show, I'd better come home with something special, or my editor is going to flay me."

"Wouldn't that be nice?"

I leaned in close. "Listen to me, lady. Find your husband, and tell him I need to speak with him. If you don't do that, you'll be sorry. I know all about the Al-Asad fragment."

When I said the words, she took a step away from me, out of her corner and against the wall.

"Who are you?" she asked, her voice rising.

"Like I said, *The Guardian.* But I've done my research."

Her eyes moved from side to side like those of a reptile deciding on fight or flight. She made the decision to go absolutely fucking bonkers.

"You won't send me back to the outer dark. I won't go! I'll kill you. I'll kill all of you lousy little PRIMATES!"

People turned to look in our direction. I shrugged and laughed. All a part of the show I guess, was the expression on my face.

This, unfortunately, drew the attention of the whole crowd who assumed, and with Frankenstein's history, who could blame them, that the real show had just started.

"I don't know what you're talking about, Miranda. I just want to talk to William. Calm down."

She screamed and slashed at my face with her nails. They were long and as sharp as razors. Blood spattered my shirt, and I let out a yelp. Everyone was watching, so I kept my hand to my face and ran for the nearest washroom. People got out of my way. They do that when you're bleeding. What Miranda did, I don't know.

By the time I'd gotten to the bathroom, the ragged gashes she'd opened had already closed. This sort of thing was impossible to explain to people. While the blood was still fresh, I applied a gauze pad from the first aid kit stashed in the lining of my coat. I'd been living with this for twenty years now. I was mostly finished by the time the first person came in to check on me.

I politely excused myself and went back into the gallery. Miranda was gone. People chattered about the blood, and when they saw me, some of them applauded. Others sniffed in disgust. One young man in an expensive suit walked right up to me.

"You," he said, "Show me your wound. I want to see the blood."

I took a step back. "No," I said. "You fucking reprobate."

I shoved past him and out into the street, looking for a taxi.

I passed an alley and felt a chill.

"Mr. Bradstreet," a familiar voice said, "you're more persistent than most of your kind. My better half tends to deflect the punters."

He was far back in the shadows, where he seemed to like it. On the video, and in his pictures, he seemed very tall, but it's often the case that when you meet people in real life they seem shorter. That was not the case here. Face to face, my first impression of him was still of his sheer enormity. Seven feet tall, and perhaps a bit more, and wide as a football player. A deep voice, but not as deep as you'd think, both sweeter and higher than my own gravel road pitch.

"Mr. Frankenstein, I presume."

He nodded slowly. "Your wound, Bradstreet, is no longer fresh. The blood is drying. I can smell it. You smell quite unusual to me in several ways. I apologize for being blunt, but you aren't exactly human are you?"

He spoke loudly enough that passersby might have heard, with no concern for any consequences at all, and it made me jittery.

"I don't know what the fuck you're on about," I said, "but as long as we're talking, would you mind giving me some time for an interview?"

He took a step forward, and his face came into view. Not as terrible as it had seemed on the video. His head was very large, and the hair lay flat around it, and uneven. One eye was larger than the other, and his lips seemed twisted in a permanent sneer by what looked like a poorly repaired cleft palate. His skin was pink as a newborn, and his eyes a pale unearthly blue.

He wore a long-sleeved shirt and leather gloves, plain black trousers, and socks with his prescription shoes.

"I don't give interviews," he said, and it sounded like a threat. "I'm not interested in fame."

"If that's so," I asked, "why are you trying so hard to get attention?"

He smiled, or I thought it was a smile. "I need no attention from the human race. I call what I do a kind of prayer. Why are you trying so very hard to hide?"

His hand came up sharply, his reach longer than I'd dreamed, and he tore the bandage from my face. My cheek was caked in dried blood, but otherwise fine.

"Not entirely human," Frankenstein said again. "Just as I thought."

"I'm human," I shouted, and then winced and spoke more quietly. "I'm human, but I have a condition."

"You talk like it's a disease. In ancient times, you'd have been worshipped as a god. Now look at you, soaked in alcohol and cringing before the wretched likes of me."

"I'm not a god, and it's not your fault you're deformed, either."

He straightened up, and looked down at me from his great height. "That word implies misfortune. I did this to myself. I was born, as it happens, quite beautiful. It's the passage of time and my own inclination that have done this to me. I choose to reflect the world in my flesh like a mirror."

"Uh-huh. I've been told to mention the Al-Asad fragment, "I said. "Does that mean anything to you?

He became very still. "It means everything to me."

"Look," I said. "If you want a frank exchange of information, I'm all for that. You might even be able to help me figure out a few things about myself. I don't want to have this conversation outside an art gallery in front of a crowd."

"Miranda is very frightened of you, and now I see why, if you mentioned the fragment."

"I had no idea it would draw that reaction."

"Obviously. You have no idea what it is do you?"

"Nope."

Frankenstein blinked. "That's surprisingly honest."

"I'm prepared to be that."

"Come to my hotel room around midnight. I'll make sure Miranda is asleep."

I took his card, a simple Black on Ivory job, no Grand Guignol excess there. He'd written his hotel and room number down with what seemed a comically undersized ballpoint.

He didn't seem half the ogre that he portrayed in his work. He was huge and he was ugly, but he was being quite polite to me. Of course, he knew I was one of the weird ones now, and I could see where he'd want to get to know me considering his fascination with the torment of the flesh.

If it weren't for the fact that MI-13 had sent Cathy to warn me, I'd have maybe felt reassured that he was just a weird kid like Marilyn Manson, selling a nightmare for kicks.

His wife still had me over in creepy crawlies. She put those terrible thoughts in my head, and aside from those thoughts I had the distinct feeling that she had no other thoughts at all. There was nobody inside her driving. I always found telepaths to be creepy, but Miranda Efrit was the worst I'd ever had to deal with. It felt like she'd wanted not just to scare me, but to corrupt me. She'd wanted to make me dirty, and then make me like it.

I had the cab drop me at a bar up the street on Commercial. I ordered a Guinness, which was on tap, sat at the bar, and listened to the crowd. I drank my beer and managed to feel a sense of bonhomie for nearly an hour. Then I had to go.

Chapter 6: The End of Flesh

Frankenstein had a much nicer hotel room than mine. This isn't intended to be a dig at the fine establishment where I was staying, and to be clear, my digs in that place were several degrees of civilization above the squalor to which I'd gotten accustomed. It's just that Frankenstein's hotel was six or seven degrees of civilization higher still.

I always feel a bit scruffy, regardless of what I'm wearing, but walking into that place in a beaten-up leather jacket drew stares. Employees in their gold and crimson uniforms turned at once, staring like a pack of wolves spotting a crippled deer. I smiled confidently and tried to look like I had a perfect right to be there. Of course, I did, and so that helped. I walked right up to the front desk.

"Excuse me," I said, laying on the accent a bit thicker than usual. "Could you let Mr. Frankenstein know that I've arrived? You'll find he's expecting me."

The near-anorectic little gay boy behind the counter typed a few keystrokes and then smiled thinly. "Just one moment, sir. Your name?"

"Tom Bradstreet."

Something hovered across his face, and he picked up the phone. "Mr. Bradstreet is at the front desk for you, sir." He placed the phone down in the cradle, and looked back at me, eyes flitting slightly, trying not to stare. "You can go right up."

"Thank you, sir," I said, tapping the counter lightly and turning to go.

"Um...are you Tom Bradstreet the writer?"

I turned back to look at him, and I could see the poor boy going over all crimson from the collar up.

"I used to be," I said, "You look now upon the dissipated remains of that man."

"*Sodomy in Gomorrah* is the book that helped me come out."

"Well, good," I said. "Closets smell of mothballs."

"I just...I'm not supposed to let on to famous people that I...Thank you."

"Lord, how I wish I was famous. You're more than welcome."

I could see him doing math in his head and wondering how I looked the way I did, and I didn't want to see him boil over.

"Must dash," I said, "He's given me an interview."

"Lucky you," said the clerk.

I winked at him and headed to the elevators, which, thank Christ, I did not have to wait for. People seldom know who I am. I am rarely, if ever, recognized. I have been asked a few times by my friends and associates how it is that I look so young. My standard response is that I live clean, no liquor and no cigarettes. Often, I've had both a drink and a cigarette in my hand as I said it.

I got off on the fifteenth floor and went down the hall. The luxurious mahogany and brass made me just the slightest bit ill. I've seen poverty, and not first world poverty. I've lived in places for months at a time where people live in squalor that most westerners actually cannot imagine. The inequity of wealth, which I benefit from as much as anyone, often strikes me as vile. Not that I'm in any rush to give out my comfort. Hypocrisy is the default state of human existence. Mankind is kept alive by monstrous acts, and all of that.

I knocked at his door, recorder in hand. He answered almost immediately. He looked down at me, his forehead actually above the level of the doorjamb.

"Mr. Bradstreet. Come in."

He was still dressed in black from head to toe, and still wearing his gloves. I walked past him, and he gracefully stood to one side.

The room was larger than most, but it was just a hotel room. There was a large bed, and a television set. By the balcony, there was a living room set and a small table with crackers and cheese on it. There was a small shelving area with a coffeemaker and a fridge and microwave. Opulent, yet dull. That struck me as something of a waste.

I looked to Frankenstein for a cue as to where he was most comfortable. He walked with head bowed to avoid lighting fixtures and gestured to the area in front of the balcony. I sat in a leather armchair, and he settled his considerable mass onto the couch. He looked visibly more at ease with the weight off of his feet.

"Much better," he said, and lifted a glass of water off the table to take a sip. "Please help yourself to whatever you might like. There is sure to be beer in the fridge over there. Serve yourself."

"Cheers," I said, not rising.

We said nothing at all for a space of ten seconds. He shifted on the couch, seemingly unable to get comfortable. I checked the battery level on my recorder.

"I'd rather you put that away," he said. "If we're to speak, I'd rather you just took notes, if you feel you must. Call it a superstition."

I shrugged, put it back in my pocket, and pulled out my pad and paper. My shorthand was rusty, but serviceable.

"As you like," I said. "Where is Miranda?"

"Elsewhere," he said. "I thought it best if the two of you didn't mingle."

"Again, cheers. No offense, but your missus is a nutter."

He laughed. "She is. I enjoy her, but she's not to all tastes."

I shrugged. "This is why ties come in different colours, mate."

His smile faded quickly from his lips. "No, that's about tribalism, but I do take your point. How did you hear about the Al-Asad?"

I smiled knowingly and leaned back in the chair. "A mutual acquaintance said I ought to mention it if I wanted to get your attention."

"The name of this mutual acquaintance?"

"She'd prefer to remain nameless."

He nodded, as though that made perfect sense to him. "So tell me, Mr. Bradstreet," he said, "what precisely is your affliction?"

I shrugged. "I don't get older, and if I get hurt, I get better in a hurry. I'm 62."

His strange blue eyes remained fixed on me in a manner I found both unwholesome and unsettling.

"So," I said, "what's yours?"

"You need to ask?" he said, gesturing to shove his misshapen body. "I was born into this world as a freak, set apart from others, but with a mind that is fierce and capable and alien."

"And Frankenstein is your real name, then?"

"It is, as it happens," he said with a smile. "Would you like to see my passport?"

I did, but I shook my head. "No thanks. May I ask your age?"

"Complicated question," he said, and nothing more.

"Right. Well, would you mind if we talked about your art?"

"I would, actually," he said. "Talking about art is like talking about masturbation. Better to simply do it."

"So, what shall we talk about then?" Frustration tainted my tone. I got the sense that he was playing with me, and had no intention of telling me anything. He was very good at deflecting inquiry.

"How did you become immortal," he asked, "and how do you feel about it?"

"The story isn't about me, William. It's about you."

"Well then, you're bound to be disappointed."

I looked at him and put my pad away. "Well, I'm sorry you feel that way, but I guess we're done here." I stood up, and he smiled.

"So soon?"

"Well, if you don't want an article I can't force it. I didn't come here to tell you all my secrets and get nothing in return."

"You know nothing of the Al-Asad, so we've both had our own false pretenses, haven't we?"

I stared at him. "I may be a liar, but at least I'm not a murderer. How did you do it?"

"Which one?" he answered.

"Your wife."

"Which time?

"You think you're pretty hard, don't you?"

"No," he said, "I'm just being honest. My wife has died many times. Lately it has been by my own hand. I'm rather hard on the things I love."

"I was referring to the film, and I think you know that."

"Oh, that. I stabbed her that time. You've seen it, I presume."

"Yes."

"Then why ask?"

I looked at him, and my temper was starting to mount. "Don't play clever bugger with me, William. You know very well what I'm asking and you know why."

"Say it, then."

"How'd you bring her back?"

"I didn't. I just helped her soul into a new body."

"Hence the name, eh?" I said smirking, and crossing my arms.

"I work in flesh, Tom. I've been clear on this from the start."

"About that," I said, "what is the deal with the show tonight?"

"Whimsy. Once in a while, it's a good idea to switch gears and leave everyone guessing."

"Why bother with all of this showing off, then? Clearly you have more on your side than just being, I'm sorry, fucking ugly. Why do all of this?"

"Art," he said. I felt he was sincere.

"Lovely. You're enriching the culture."

"Everyone is so obsessed with death and decay, but nobody appreciates it. It's beautiful. Being denied it, I'd think you'd appreciate the allure."

"You'd think wrong."

"À chacun à son goût," he said, shrugging.

"Cheers," I said.

"Before you leave," he said, "would you mind giving me a demonstration?"

"A demonstration?"

"Of your gift," he said.

"You want me to bleed for you, is that it?"

"Would you mind very much?"

I glared at him. "Be fucked," I said, and started for the door.

He laughed and rose from his couch. It was almost polite.

"By the way," I said, "I was asked to give you a message. They want you to quit all of this art nonsense and go back to just being a creeper in the dark. They don't want you to deform the social order."

"The social order? Hardly the sentiments of the man standing before me. I wouldn't have pegged you as a lackey to the powers that be."

"Me neither, but what can I say, I just don't like you, mate."

"A shame," he said, "in another life we might have been friends." I goggled at the pure and unrestrained cliché of him. "Tell your keepers that their social order is already doomed. The world is two meals from savagery, and in any case, a monster that dwarfs my small ambitions is coming for us all. The death ship is blowing in from the outer dark."

I had my hand on the knob, and turned back. "The what?"

"The death ship. From the Al-Asad." He smiled smugly.

"You're one of those, then, are you?" I said, and walked slightly closer.

"One of what?" he answered.

"Apocalyptics. People who have a hard on for summoning monsters to end the world."

"End the world?" Frankenstein said, taken aback, "Oh no. Nothing will end the world. The world will be just fine. The end of flesh, on the other hand is a consummation most devoutly to be wished."

"The nice thing," I said, "about indestructibility is that it comes in handy."

I reached behind me for my knife. "If you want an end to flesh, you just stand still."

His eyes went wide and he stood with his hands on his hips.

I slashed across his body with the knife, going for his throat, but cutting across his chest instead. A weak trickle of dark blood spilled down the front of his shirt. I did not get a second chance. His fists closed around my wrists and squeezed until the bones snapped. He picked me up off the ground with a terrible swiftness and ease, and shook me for a moment before dropping me. I felt like a rat in the mouth of a terrier.

Every inch of me hurt as he stood over me and knelt to pick up my knife. I tried to roll to my hands and knees, but my wrist hadn't knitted well enough to support weight yet. He put his heavy foot on my neck and, like a child playing with lawn darts, tossed the knife down into my eye. Mumblety-Peg.

I went dark for a few minutes. When I came back to myself, he was resting on his haunches watching my eye heal, and weeping.

"I wish my father could have seen this."

"Fuck your father," I said, spitting up into his lopsided face.

He wiped the spittle from his face. "Children," he said, "come out."

I heard the sound of skittering and shuffling, and turned my head to the side to see what he called children. I screamed.

An eyeball with a blown pupil had been grafted to a human hand, mounted on the tail of a scorpion, which, in turn, was attached to the stump of a wrist. As it crawled up my face I could see the open mouth of a frog grafted somehow into the palm. Its long tongue flicked out and tasted me.

A pair of torsos had been grafter together like some multi-segmented insect, crawling on four arms. No head was in sight, but the open neck was covered in a membrane that flicked open and shut like the eyelid of some huge thing. A revolt of flesh, which crawled on the bed and the rug and every available surface.

I couldn't move. My limbs felt like lead, my skin numb.

Miranda walked from the closet. She was nude, and I could see the scars where he had put her together piece by piece. She picked up a human head, eyelids sewn shut, grafted to a large slug, and she kissed it with tongue, her other hand sliding down to the mass of cilia at her crotch. They waved like anemone. I was grateful when the blackness came.

Chapter 7: No Business I Know

I woke up in chains like King Kong. A great manacle around my neck held me to the wall, and cuffs at my ankles and my wrists were heavy enough that my urge to struggle waned quickly. When I craned my head slightly, I found myself in a black room with theatre lighting. I was still dressed the same way, but the front of my shirt was even bloodier than I remembered. It looked as though Frankenstein and his children had played with me a little more.

I took care to breathe evenly, and tried to listen hard. The furnace was ticking away, and

I thought I could hear talking in the next room, but I wasn't certain. Our brains like to play that trick on us. The way my head was chained meant I couldn't see much past my own chest. I wasn't desperate enough yet to skin my own hand to get out of the cuffs. It wouldn't help, if I couldn't get my head free. I wasn't brave enough to try anything foolish with my head.

Frankenstein came into the room a moment later, with a clipboard in his hand. On either side of him were two men who looked like backstage technicians. Long hair in ponytails, scruffy jeans, and tool belts. He directed them as to the positioning of lights. When he realized I was awake, he excused himself and came over to me.

"Hello Tom," he said. "I trust you're feeling better?"

"Take these fucking chains off of me, or I swear to god I'm going to make you sorry."

He acted as if he hadn't heard me speak at all. "You're really a fascinating creature."

He took off his glove and showed me his right hand. My right hand.

It turns out that I really could recognize the back of my own hand. I could see the livid stitches where he'd sewn it to his wrist. I had nothing readily to say about that.

"It took seven tries to graft one on but, happily, your hand just kept growing back so I could try again and again."

I wriggled my own hand, feeling the fingers move. "It does that."

He nodded solemnly.

"You cut off your own hand?" I asked.

"I had some help, but yes."

"How long was I out?"

"Just a day. I thought it was best to keep you under while I did my explorations."

"Thanks."

Frankenstein put his glove back on and went back over to the workmen. After a few minutes, they left, and Frankenstein sat on the bench seating across the stage from me. He crossed a leg over and massaged the calf.

"It's not easy to be so damnably tall," he said. "Pain. All the time. And unlike my darling wife, I've not developed a taste for it.

"Have you considered suicide?"

"Of course not. The show must go on. For one thing, it's a mortal sin. For another, my creator endowed me with a fierce tenacity and a desire to stay alive. My natural instinct for self-preservation would never allow me to walk into a blast furnace, nor to stand by while some tiny man with a knife tried to cut my throat. No matter how much I can see it's for the best. No, and more's the pity, I have a taste for vengeance."

"Well, that's great. You intend to torture me, then? I've been tortured before. I was even tortured a couple of times when it still left scars."

Frankenstein rested his entire weight back on his long arms, his legs straight out before him. "I saw that, yes. I don't torture people. It's pointless. I'm only interested in exploring their limits. I don't know what it would take to actually destroy you, but I am interested. Aren't you?"

"No. You know what interests me? Beer. Sex. A good book. A good movie. A good laugh. That's more or less the whole lot. Anything else I can take or leave."

"Simple tastes," he said. "Mine too."

"So what is all this then?" I asked, trying to gesture with my head.

"I'm preparing for an impromptu show before we leave Vancouver. It's all very last minute, but I had to strike while the iron was hot."

MI-13 might still have half an eye on me. Heather was expecting a call and Lisa was expecting me home on Sunday. It wasn't much hope. But even the smallest drop is something when you're shitting your pants in terror.

"I'm part of the show, I presume."

"Of course."

"Is there a script I should memorize or anything?"

"The piece will work best if you are entirely surprised."

"What's it called?" I asked, trying to be conversational, and trying not to give him the pleasure inherent in seeing me panic.

"Violet Swarm."

My heart pounded in my chest.

"Do excuse me," he said, and he left. I realized that his mind-raping bitch intended to make all of my dreams come true. I screamed. I screamed again. I continued screaming, literally ad nauseam. The vomit was bloody from my irritated throat.

I sagged limply in my chains.

"How were the levels on that?" Frankenstein asked someone in the hall.

"Fine," was the reply.

Miranda came in the room, dressed in a man's suit with a vest. She came right up to me and jabbed the needle in my neck. I didn't mind. I fell into a dark and dreamless place.

Time had no meaning for me whatsoever. It might have been an hour later, or it might have been a year. Three people stood in front of me, staring. One of them was a rather famous Canadian filmmaker, known for making films nearly as obsessed with flesh as Frankenstein himself. He moved his thick black frames down his nose slightly to get a better look at something.

"That," he said, "really is remarkable. Do it again."

I felt a sharp pain in my chest, and some blood misted up onto my chin. A little spattered his glasses. I couldn't see who'd cut me.

"Fuckers," I said, my voice slurring. "Kill all of you lousy primates."

"Jesus! He's awake," the filmmaker said, jerking back suddenly, and hiding his face.

"Don't be like that," came Frankenstein's voice over the sound system. "After all, Tom, you're my right-hand man."

A small tittering laugh came from around my knees. I couldn't see what made it, but there was another hypodermic pinch, and I went down into the dark again.

I don't name the filmmaker for two reasons. For one, I don't want to be sued. For the other, I don't know for certain it was any more than a dream.

The next thing that I remember was a calliope playing, and the sound of seagulls. I saw Frankenstein step past me and into the light.

The rest of the performance I don't recall. Yet. I'm sure it'll come one day. I'm waiting.

CHAPTER 8: INTERMISSION

The alley I woke up in was muddy, and so was I. Rain was still coming down hard. I coughed up a lungful of muddy water and followed it with some bile.

I leaned against the wet and crumbling brick, dressed in jeans and a black t-shirt. My own clothes, and my treasured leather jacket, were gone. God only knows what was left of it, if anything. I didn't know where I was, nor did I know what had happened, and here I was, half grieving for a piece of dead cow skin.

I walked out into the street, East Hasting unsurprisingly. If you're going to dump somebody someplace in Vancouver, it's a fine choice. My wallet was in my pocket, so I kept walking until I was in a neighbourhood where the cabs would stop.

I went up to the front desk at my hotel, still soaking wet.

"Could I get a key to my room please. I seem to have lost it."

"Of course," said the clerk. "What's your name?"

"Bradstreet," I said, "Room 211."

She frowned. "Where have you been?"

"I was robbed."

"You've been missing for days. The police have been in your room and everything. They have all of your things impounded. Someone else has your room now, and...." She looked at me, saw the trauma, and her voice softened.

"Jesus," she said, "Listen to me. You should sit down. The police will want to talk to you." I stared at her, not sure what I needed to do next. "Sir," she said again, "are you listening to me?"

By now two of her coworkers had come by to look at me.

"No way," said the tall, broadly built one with the red-brown goatee. "No way is that guy still alive, no matter what kind of freak he is."

"What was that?" I asked, snapping out of it.

"I saw what happened to you on YouTube, man. No way was that a special effect."

I turned and ran out the front of the hotel. I ran until I had no earthly idea where I was. I'd only visited Vancouver a couple of times. I found a bus shelter to get out of the rain and tried to think about my situation.

How had I gotten away from Frankenstein? I couldn't imagine he'd have just decided he was done with me. I didn't think he would tire of me any time soon. What had happened in my missing time? I didn't like the thought of it being on YouTube. Was my life as a normal person, living under the radar over for good?

I thought back to the night at my place when Lisa had come over, and I was cooking a stir-fry. She distracted me, and I took the tip of my middle finger off with the knife. She screamed. Then, a few seconds later, while she was mothering me and she saw my flesh knitting itself back together, she screamed again. It was a week, a solid week, before she spoke to me. I tried to explain it to her, but it was hard to, not really understanding it myself. Gradually we stopped fussing, and life got back to normal. I doubted that the rest of the world would be so easygoing.

I went looking for a phone booth. They're a dying breed, but I eventually found one. I had no change so I put my credit card into it. It was a silly thing to do. So, probably, was the next thing I did. I called Lisa. The phone rang six times, and I was about to hang up when the phone came up off the hook on the other end.

She sounded terrible, and also as if I'd woken her up, which I had. It was the dead of night.

"Whozit?" she said.

"It's me."

"Tom!" she said. "Oh my god. Where are you?"

"Vancouver still. I..."

"Are you okay? The police told me that you were...."

"I'll live," I said. "I always do, Christ."

"They say you were killed. It's all over the Internet, but I...I couldn't watch it."

"Takes more than bad art to finish me off, pet."

She sniffled on the other end of the line.

"I'm okay," I said. "I'm wet, and sore and just a bit scared. Tell me, am I all over the news as some kind of freak?"

"No. I mean, I don't think so. Apparently Frankenstein was saying you were, but everybody thinks it's just part of the show."

I sighed with relief. It still meant I'd have to take some steps, but I hadn't been exactly outed.

"The landlord," she said, "won't let the cops in your place without a warrant. But they say they're coming back with one."

"Use your key," I said. "Hide my porn."

"Shut up."

"But what of my reputation?"

She laughed, snorting back her tears. "Are you sure you're okay?"

"For now, yes. I may not be back for a while, but I'll stay in touch. I need to talk to some of my old friends."

"Oh," she said. "From the old days you don't talk about?"

"Yes."

She was silent. "Am I safe?"

"There's a couple thousand dollars in the tobacco tin in the back of my fridge. I'd like you to take it, and be elsewhere for a while.

Try Dublin. Dublin's really nice in the autumn."

She knew better than to think she had to ask me twice about money.

"Tom," she said, "I..."

"Stay safe," I said and hung up the phone. I leaned against it for a few minutes.

I went out into the night again, and looked for another pay phone. I found one just inside an all-night breakfast place. I sat down and ordered a bowl of hot tomato soup with extra crackers, and a sandwich. I dialed Heather's office, and left her a message. I told her I'd try to call again soon, and that I was alive and well, no matter what she saw on Wikipedia.

I ate the bowl of soup and absently stuffed the extra crackers in my pockets. I grew up poor. I do things like that without thinking. On my way out I bought a two-liter bottle of Diet Pepsi and headed out again. The sun had started to come up, and the rain was dying off to a slight trickle. I drank from the neck of the bottle, the caffeine adding slight clarity to my thought processes.

I found a cheap motel, paid in cash, then staggered to my room and laid face down on the bed.

The police woke me up about an hour later, pounding on the door. I said nothing as they came into the place. I said nothing as they asked me where I'd been. I said nothing as they put me in the back of the car and started to drive. I said nothing once I got to the station except to say that I wanted a lawyer.

When my lawyer came, he told me that I'd committed no crime, and the cops had laid no charges. They just wanted to know if I knew where William S. Frankenstein was.

"I have no fucking idea, Christ. He kidnapped me and he drugged me, and he apparently put me on public exhibit. When he was done with me, he dumped me in the worst place in town."

"Well," the lawyer said, "if it makes you feel any better, the police are certainly looking for him. He broke all kinds of laws, and apparently Interpol is involved now."

"Do they have anything to hold me on?" I asked. "Anything at all?"

"Not really, but they could think of something. They might charge you as an accessory to the crimes done during the show, but if they do, they'll have a hard time proving anything. You're sure you have no idea what happened?"

"Nothing," I said. "From the moment I drank that glass of water in Frankenstein's hotel room, it's a blank."

Lying is fun. Everyone should do it.

"If your priority," my lawyer said, "is leaving, I can help with that. If you just get up and go, they're going to manufacture some kind of charge to justify questioning you. I recommend we draft a written statement that gives a full run down."

We did that, and he warned that, while this would get me on the street, the cops would not be happy.

In fact, the cops were not happy. They never are unless you present them with a full solution to the crime, all tied up with a bow. I shook my lawyer's hand, with actual gratitude, and got the hell out of Dodge.

I was sitting in the airport departures lounge, reading a magazine, and looking very much forward to just going home and coping with all of the consequences Frankenstein had left for me. If MI-13 called me, I'd cooperate fully. At some point, I'd even look into exactly what that performance had entailed. Just then, I found it hard to care. I only wanted to sleep in my own bed.

Miranda sat down beside me. dressed like half of the people in the building, jeans and a t-shirt. Her long hair pulled into a ponytail through the back of a ball cap. She had dark glasses on.

"Hello Tom," she said. "Sorry to lead you on. We had to dump you for a short while, just in case they found us."

"Fuck you, bitch," I said, softly.

"Oh you DO remember the show?"

"Happily fucking not, but the name was sufficiently evocative, thanks very much."

"The Dermestid beetles all died. We don't know if it was from feeding on your unnatural flesh, or the purple paint. It's a pity though," she said.

"What do you want?" I said, interrupting her before she went into any further detail.

"The redheaded boy we hired choked to death when William cut out his tongue," she said, smiling.

"SHUT UP!" I screamed, and people turned to look at us.

"Calm yourself."

"What do you want?" I asked again.

"You're going to come with me, out to the car, and then all of us are getting on a boat."

"The hell I am, and the hell we are."

"Tom," she said softly, "I learned a lot about what hurts you during that brief moment of intimacy. Far more than you know of what may hurt me. If you don't come with me, William will do things to Lisa, your...protégé, that you can't imagine. Unlike you, or I, she won't survive it. Unless he chooses her as my next host. The bone structure is a bit different, but William is a genius with a knife, and the scars never did quite heal this time."

I swallowed hard. "Why are you doing this to me?"

"I tried to scare you off. And then you tried to scare me. I didn't like that, darling. And then? You tried to kill him. That was a very bad mistake. It means that he simply adores you now, and it means that he wants you to hurt. If you'd just walked away, you'd have been left alone. There are rules when dealing with him."

She patted my knee. "You'll learn to love pain eventually, I'm sure."

I slapped her hand off of me like a dropped cigarette. "Let's go," I said, standing up.

She stood up as well and put her hand on the small of my back to steer me.

"Stop fucking touching me," I said, "or as god's my witness I'll end you."

"Melodrama," she said. "Tiresome. You've nothing to threaten me with but a good time." She steered me to the arrivals lounge and to a limousine waiting for us.

William was lying across one entire bench seat, dressed in a tuxedo, his platform boot shined to a high polish. A top hat rested in his lap.

"Hello Tom," he said. "Sorry about all the risen hopes. Do get in."

I did. What choice did I have?

Miranda leaned across the aisle and kissed him hello. The two of them made small talk about the weather, and what the conditions were apt to be at sea.

After half an hour, we pulled into a trucking facility, and I was ushered into a shipping container.

"What the hell is going on?"

"We're taking a trip, as Miranda no doubt told you. You're traveling as cargo. There's a bucket in there for your usage. No provisions, though. It's time for you to fully embrace what you are. You'll live. You always do."

I tried to run, but he tossed me into the dark with no more effort than a child tossing a doll into a toybox.

"See you soon," he said, and he and his horrible wife laughed at the look on my face as they sealed the door with a metallic clanging.

Chapter 9: And So

I think of the thousand ways I could have handled my brief moments of freedom with more cleverness and dignity. I think of all the mistakes I've ever made. I wonder how my sweet ginger boy's self-inflicted madness caused this change in my flesh. I wonder how magic works. I walk back and forth in this tiny cage and try to ignore the heat and the smell of days-old shit. I try to think of what it is that I will do from this point out. I wonder if Lisa is all right, and Heather. And if Carter and his husband know I'm missing, and I hope they do, because if they do, then the Sideshow will soon hear about it.

I wonder if the Sideshow let this happen to me as a kind of petty punishment, a reminder of why I need them more than they need me.

I wonder if it's possible to go insane from suffering, and if, in the long run Victor did me no favours. A million years of life ahead, and I was forgetting what it was like to not suffer.

I wonder what it is that makes William S. Frankenstein tick, and what exactly the thing he calls his wife might be. I wonder if there will be any answers to my questions. I wonder if I care.

I think about my father, and his callused hands as they held the belt before lashing me. "It's a hard life," he said, "and best you learn to behave from me than some of the monsters out there." I'm grateful because he taught me to shut my eyes and forget my body. In this dark, hot, dry box, that is a useful damned skill indeed.

I wonder if he's still alive, and I think of his drinking and smoking, and I know the answer in my bones like cancer. It aches that I still love him like crazy no matter how many scars he laid across my back.

I think of that damned island where Victor made his damned bargain for my life. Sel Souris, where the purple beetles swarm, and where it seems half the magic in the world comes from. I wish I'd never heard of it.

I think of the few other immortals I'd found and how none of them were like I was. Whatever it was that kept them alive lived in the blood somewhere and could be passed along. I remember the advice of the hundred-and thirty-year-old cowboy telling me I should try it on Victor.

I think of pressing the pillow to Victor's face when it didn't work, and making sure that he was dead.

I think of drinking and of drinking and of drinking and of drinking.

Which makes me thirstier, and so I stop.

I think of William S. Frankenstein and the sickness that drives him. I hate him and I pity him at the same time. He's terrifying and dangerous, and he seems so very sad and sorry. I am not sure what he wants with me, but I know that I want no part of it.

I am so thirsty.

As twisted and strange as my own flesh is, and as my life has become, I love life. I can still make friends. And I think of Lisa, with her sadness I don't understand, and the sweetness of her, and the loneliness that bonds us. I think of the children I'll never have, and while I'd hope mine would be happier, I expect they'd turn out like her. I would not regret that.

I hope my sudden disappearance doesn't turn her further away from people.

I begin to think that I should plan for not making it out of this. I wonder if a fire would kill me given time and persistence.

I think about scooping a handful of my own muck out of the bucket just for the moisture, and I control myself by millimeters.

I realize how much of life is like that. We avoid the worst choices by the skin of our teeth—dignity and hope, and a kind of mad optimism that it'll get better in a few minutes. That it MUST, it just has to get better.

When the bolts slide back, I have less than five seconds to close my eyes before the light streams in. I'm so dizzy that I hadn't noticed the container moving. The light, even through my eyelids, feels like someone pressing a hot brand to the underside of my brain. The air rushes in, cool on my skin, and I nearly faint from pure relief.

"My god," Frankenstein says, "you're beautiful."

This almost certainly means that I look like a desiccated corpse, and I might as well be one.

On either side of him are two Asian men in khaki uniforms. They have green caps on, and are armed with AK-47 assault rifles. I blink my dry eyes, no longer filmed with tears, and I see that they have a red star, surrounded by two sheaves. They're North Korean soldiers.

My life has become, officially, completely insane.

In a car surrounded by soldiers, is Kim Jong-Il, the sole dictator of North Korea. He sees me step out into the sun, and then turns to his driver, and they drive away, soldiers jogging along beside as it makes slow progress down the road.

I try to speak to Frankenstein, but can make no more than a ragged croak. He turns to one of the soldiers and says something in what I assume is Korean. The soldier nods briskly and speaks on his walkie-talkie. Despite his immediate obedience, pure panic hides behind his eyes.

Frankenstein offers me an arm. I had planned on running, but I'd not thought about the effects of being so long in the dark, and I'm weaker than I'd even imagined. His hands, one of which used to be mine, are gentle as he helps me to a nearby bench and sits me down.

A woman in uniform jogs up and hands me a canteen. The water smells incredible, and it tastes better. I take small sips, not huge gulps. I know that's safest.

Frankenstein smiles, pleased. "Good. Not too much at first."

"What," I say, choking a little, as my tissues soak in the water like a sponge, "do you care?"

He inclines his head. "I know your limits now. I don't need you to suffer."

"Hooray."

I pour the water over my head, and my skin visibly plumps up. One of the soldiers gasps out loud, and covers his mouth. Frankenstein merely smiles. The surface of my skin is dry again, and I take another sip of the water, nearly emptying the canteen.

"More," I say.

Frankenstein looks at the woman, and she nods, taking the canteen and jogging off. The soldiers here don't walk anywhere they don't have to, it would seem.

She is back in less than a minute, and I drink some more. My head stops ringing. "Are you well enough to travel?" he asks me.

"That depends on where."

"My home."

"Am I your little pet, now? Is that it? I'm not a very good one. I've got diseases, you know. I bite."

William claps a hand on my shoulder. "Tom. I need you. I'll explain everything once you've had some food and some rest. A mansion, and all the material luxuries in the world await us, provided we give Kim what he needs."

"And what's that?"

"Immortality. After all, he's only dictator for life."

I stare at him, and I know he thinks it's funny. It's absurd, even, but he means it too, and he's game to try. He is living his life by his wits and his perversity, and he seems happy, his smile genuine. There is no malice in his eyes for the first time since I've met him. He is living his best life.

A car takes us to a large house in the hills. I am escorted to a large bedroom with bars on the window. I hear the doors as they lock behind me. Sleep on a soft mattress is all I can think about. I am half asleep by the time I slide my legs between the sheets, and all the way gone as my head hits the pillows.

Chapter 10: Striptease

Three days later, I have smoked six packs of cigarettes, and drunk six quarts of single malt scotch. Nothing has been denied me, and I've indulged. Why not? There are guards every place I turn. I'm a prisoner. I might as well be a drunken, satiated one. I'm not proud. The guards are accommodating, but keep a slight distance from me, as though they are frightened of me, or that what I have that makes him so interested in me might be catching.

I have not seen Miranda since our arrival. He knows how revolting I find her, and he's pampering me, trying to get in my good graces. He's checked up on me each day, and told me that this coming weekend, the dictator wishes to see a demonstration of my healing ability. I know that I have no choice, and so does Frankenstein, but he does seem at least slightly apologetic. He doesn't involve me in his conversations with the soldiers or white coats, and that's fine. I can't understand what they're saying, and I like to watch. Everyone is terrified of him, but just as polite as can be. They are all of them caught between their duty and a demon in platform shoes. Either he enjoys it, or hasn't noticed because they're just normal people, and barely worth attention.

I spend my days thinking of ways to murder him, but I have my suspicion that he's no more likely to die than I am. I don't ask. I show no interest of any kind. He does not probe.

Today he comes in, and he wears no gloves. In fact, he is wearing only a bathrobe. He carries a cane, and he needs it to walk because his one leg is so much shorter. His feet are bare.

I have never seen so much exposed skin on him. I assumed he was ashamed of his scars. He sits down on a chair by my bed, lets out a small groan of pain.

"I beg your pardon, Tom," he says, "but I think it's time to talk."

"Do we have to?"

"You see," he says, "I still don't know if you truly don't know your own story, or if you are keeping it secret for reasons of your own. I feel that by telling you my own, you might be motivated to tell me, if only for reasons of your own self-preservation."

"More threats. Christ. You don't even know how to talk to other people do you? One second it's all solicitation and compliments, and the next you make demands and veiled threats. What is wrong with you? What in the hell is going on in that brain of yours?"

He nods. "My thoughts have always been unusual, my mood swings dramatic, and it's only gotten worse as I've continued my work. I'm made up of so many people, that consistency may be too much to expect of me."

"If you want to tell me your story go ahead. The bad guy always does. Just know that I've heard a lot of stories from narcissists and sociopaths all around the world, and the one thing you've all got in common is that you think you're more interesting than you are. You're a low rent Bond villain. At best."

He smiles. "Where shall I start?"

"Tell me your fucking name, then. Your pseudonym annoys the piss out of me."

He stands up, and he drops his robe. His skin is a chaotic smear of different shades, and he looks more like a quilt than a man. A patch of flesh on his right pectoral is midnight Nigerian black, and just below it, swathed over the navel is Nordic pale, and as hairy as the pelt of a bear. His right arm is mismatched, the shoulder to the elbow is thick and tanned, and the elbow to the wrist seems Asian. The hand is the one he cut off of me. His legs have come from two different men altogether. One hip is tattooed, the other scarred and beaten, and looks like it came from a woman. He has a partial labia, of one piece with the woman's hip and pelvis, and nestled above it, buried in a mass of scar tissue, visible beneath the curly mat of pubic hair, a small and wormish cock that's all out of proportion to his massive size. Is any of that functional? I don't care to speculate but, of course, I do.

He turns in a circle, showing me all of him, and all of his scars. "My name," he says, "is Frankenstein."

Chapter 11: The Confession of William S. Frankenstein

My name is Frankenstein; or rather that was my father's name. He gave me no name, aside from one casual remark in which he may have called me Adam. I've never known for certain. Once language was mine, I held to that particular name with a sad desperation. I had no friends, no home, no simple humanity, but I had a name. I was Adam, first of my new and terrible kind.

My father was a brilliant man with, I soon discovered, more passion than wisdom, more intelligence than mercy, and more cowardice than loyalty. He pieced me together from pieces of dead men, stitching me into a single form. The method by which he animated me was not scientific as we would understand that term, but alchemical. He had, partially on the strength of his reputation, come into possession of a material which granted him the ability to transmute gold from lead, and to instill life into dead flesh. My flesh contains traces of this substance. Time and Miranda's assistance have helped me distill it in small quantities. I use it to play.

I was not, at first, monstrous to look at. His handiwork was delicate, and his stitching that of a master cobbler. My face, my face was the only problem. The blow to the head that killed my donor had deformed my skull, not so severely as it now appears, but badly enough that even after his repairs, one could not mistake me for a normal man. But I was not monstrous.

I was tall and strong. The chemicals that saturated my body caused my varied nerves and tissues to combine without revolting one against the other. It also granted me a vitality that was superhuman. Its work on my mental processes, repairing the damaged brain was much slower.

You know the story, I think. Indeed, what schoolchild does not? My father was horrified by the powers he had commanded, and in terror of his new found godhood, rejected me, and all responsibility for me. I fled to the woods and learned the ways of men at a remote distance. I took their cruelties as my first and most important lesson.

In the end of the story, as recorded by Captain Walton, and then by Mary Shelley, I set myself adrift with my father's body so that both of us should die in the northern wastes. It was a finer ending than the truth, and I don't blame them for it. They were romantics.

In truth, as I've said before, I could never willingly consign myself to the grave. The vital forces in me are too strong. In my weakest moments I have considered suicide, but my own hands rebelled against it every time. Know this, I have, in my soul, ached for an end for a long time.

My father and I drifted on the ice for a long time, long after his death from the cold. I was cold also and hungry, but did not die. In time, men found me. Indians of the far north. At that time they were called Esquimaux by white men. I've since discovered that name to be a regrettable slander. I stayed with them for a time. While they were kind to me, and found my prowess as a hunter useful, I was never one of them. I wandered south, and lived like a wild man. I hunted small game for food, and occasionally stole clothing and food from homes, staying always far as I could from men.

Fifty years or more passed, and one morning, I discovered my left foot was dead. It had no feeling, and while it would support my weight, it was falling apart like a ruined shoe. I worried that, at long last, I was facing my mortality.

In the woods of Virginia, desperately limping and in fear for my life, I came upon a group of three escaped slaves. They panicked and one of them attempted to stab me. I crushed them with my bare hands as though they were toys. I stood in the carnage annoyed and ashamed when the idea first came upon me.

I took the knife and cut off the largest man's foot slightly above the ankle. Even with my strength, it was hard work with his dull blade. Then I set to the same task with my dead foot. The pain was terrible, but not sufficient to forestall me. Pain holds none of the urgency for me that it does for normal men of woman born. I am jealous of this, as I am of so many things.

In my satchel I had needle and thread to repair my ragged clothing. I sewed skin to skin. The fit was poor, and I could not stand on it for several days. I sat beside the mouldering corpses and watched as this poor innocent's foot became my own. After a week I could stand. A few days later, I could walk.

Philosophy, in those days, was my only entertainment. I was responsible now, in part, for my own murder. What part of that man was left alive in me, I wondered? Where in the flesh does spirit reside? My own head once belonged to another man. His friends knew his face. I knew no part of this life. Was I myself, or only him, suffering from some tragic amnesia? I did not know.

I knew though, if nothing else, that my flesh would endure. Like a machine now, if my parts wore out I could replace them, and indeed I have done so becoming the man, or men before you. In those days, I sought a clean fit and a good match. That would change over time as my taste became eclectic. Variety is the spice of life. So is fear.

I returned to Europe by enlisting in the Great War. Once I arrived, I simply ran away.

There was only a burned wreck where my father's home once stood, and a young family turning it to a farm. I went back into the woods. Lacking any nation to call my own, and any vocation, I followed an acquaintance into the French Foreign Legion, fighting as a soldier for pay.

I was very good at this, and amassed money for the first time. I made some friends as well, or friendly acquaintances perhaps. After my service, one of them helped me invest that money. Simple compound interest has done much work for me, but so too has careful investment. Also, discovering the ease that money lent my life, I began to acquire it voraciously through murder and theft, investing carefully.

My life became comfortable and isolated. I read constantly, branching out from the philosophers to those who wrote fiction. It was in this period that I discovered the records of Captain Walton had survived, and that a book had been written of my life. Moreover, the book had been quite popular, and had been adapted into several films. I found this darkly funny and continued to go under the name of Adam Frankenstein regardless. Most were too polite to say a word, and some assumed it was an affectation. Either satisfied me.

I discovered the writing of Joyce and found most interesting his attempts to capture on paper the workings of the human mind. My own mind did not flit so much from topic to topic, was not so wrapped in layers of metaphor. My thoughts were direct, pure, and non- contradictory. As others took up the craft of stream of consciousness, I began to understand the vagaries of men.

More interesting was the work of the Beats. Vulgar and raw, they did not shy from the open sewer of the mind. Their ambitions, too, were greater. More than stories, more than simply portraying the actual state of things, some of these writers were after some new kind of perception altogether.

I was in Tangiers in the late fifties. Many writers traveled there, some staying months at a time. To them I was an eccentric German tourist. They asked me what I'd done during the war, and I told them I'd read Voltaire. I knew Tangiers well, having been there often since my days as a Legionnaire, and I showed them the sights, the best clubs. The fleshpots and the drugs were always their primary interest. It was in Tangiers that I met the American writer William S. Burroughs.

Born to a dissipating but wealthy family, the inventors of the adding machine, I think, and alienated not only from them but also from nearly everybody since he was a child. A drug addict and a homosexual, he traveled sometimes under the name William Lee. He assumed my name was a nom de guerre just as his was, and this delighted him.

A sly observer, and soft-spoken, with a low and raspy voice not very different from your own, he found me fascinatingly ugly. I found him to be both good company and unerringly polite and kind. His views on the ways of men were similar to mine. Like me, he looked at much of human behaviour as a smokescreen to distract them from the oozing and pulsing of their various holes, the deep and messy parts of being an animal.

He was ashamed of nearly everything he did, and every pleasure he took, and yet he plunged on, haunted by regret. His mind was as cold and bright as any crystal.

Some years later we met again in Paris, where he was living in a terrible hotel.

In that hotel room one night, both of us having smoked a great deal of hashish, he made love with me. It was the first time any creature had shown me such tenderness. In his low, suggestive, very American voice, he asked me the origin of each scar. I lied many stories for him. He called me his monster, and his fingers traced the places where my father's stitches were their crudest. He saw me naked, and I suspect he knew there was more to my name than whimsy, for by this time, I had replaced many pieces of myself.

I returned to Germany a few days later and did not see him face to face again.

We stayed in communication for the rest of his life. We wrote long letters. He was old fashioned in this regard. Later he began to send audio tapes to me, some with his voice alone, and some with his friend Gysin, simply discussing those parts of their philosophies I found most fascinating. They pioneered, you know, a kind of writing called the cut up. He took newspapers, or paragraphs of his own devising, and cut them up with razors. He would place these back together in different orders, mixing sources and he would record the result. He felt that by combining and recombining these varied elements he might get subliminal hints of the future, or a deeper, if alien, understanding of the present.

What was I but this concept given flesh? I began to replace my parts even before they gave out, selecting mismatched and variegated tones. When I looked in the mirror at my deformity I saw mankind as a whole, and I began, as I think Bill did, to understand flesh just as his gave up for good.

I had found, in his friendship, a kind of peace for a time. And in tribute to him and his cutups, I merged his name with mine.

I became William S. Frankenstein. I began to experiment with the limits of my body, and the force that animated it. I began to inject dead tissue with my blood, my tears, and finally my spinal fluid to see what would happen.

My spinal fluid, it seemed, contained some measure of my animating substance. The first of my children were a human hand that crawled, for a short time, blindly across the carpet of my bedroom and a frog, which hopped twice and croaked before falling still. It took many years before I learned to concentrate the essence from my tissue properly.

For a time, I experimented with the grafting of animal skin and flesh to my own. It was easy, but it made too difficult my passing through human society in even the limited way that I chose to.

Shortly after Bill's passing, I received a phone call from a lawyer. He informed me that William had left some few items in a box, and that they wished to arrange for me to have them. I made those arrangements immediately.

On the top of the box was a letter from my Bill.

Chapter 12: A Letter Sent from the Western Lands

My dear Monster,

Off the coast of Gibraltar, isolated from damned near any other piece of land whatsoever is a small island called Sel Souris. You may have heard of the place. Considering your travels, and how damned strange you are, it would surprise me somewhat if you had not.

I try to visit the place every few years, which is easy enough for me as a cock-sucking Amurrican. They don't let colonials on the island, which probably includes you, and most especially includes you if you're really German, about which I have strong doubts. I go because I find the people there to be the most disagreeable on Earth, because there is damned close to no kind of law there at all, and because they stay the hell out of your business. I also go because they have a drug made from the glands of a beetle that is unlike anything I've ever put in my body. It does things to a human brain that might more rightly be left to the province of the Gods. The island has got nothing else, but of beetles they have plenty. The ground is thick with them. You get used to sliding around in their guts, and everyone there is sharing some kind of low-level unity high. The drug is telepathic, I think, and it changes you. It's a million times better than Yage, and I sometimes regret I wasted a lot of time tramping in jungles in South America.

Last year, I went for what will turn out to be my last time, I suspect. When I was there, I met a woman named Miranda. She recognized me and insisted on speaking with me, even though I was quite clearly trying to read a book. As you know, I find it damned near impossible to be rude to a person no matter how much they are imposing upon my privacy, and we started to talk.

She told me that she was three hundred years old, and that she was a kind of parasite that made its living by jumping from one human body into another. She was, she said, an ardent fan of my work, that when she first read The Ticket That Exploded, she felt understood for the first time.

You have to understand, and in fact I'm sure you do, that I endure this kind of tiresome nonsense with some regularity. People seem to think they need to work overtime to be interesting to me. It's exhausting and demoralizing, but I suppose it's nice to be recognized. Anyway. She knew that I had spent a lot of time in Interzone, and she asked me if I had met a German there named Frankenstein. This piqued my interest, and I said that, as a matter of fact, I had.

She clapped her hands, and demanded I tell her all about you.

I told her that you had shown me and Ginsberg around a few places, and you and I had talked, and said nothing of any real consequence. A gentleman never tells, except in his filthy books.

She told me then that she knew your father, the famous scientist Victor Frankenstein, the one from the book. The book, she said, was true, but by no means was it the full story, and that I was a lot closer than I knew to the truth about the Nova Mob and the Nova Heat. She asked if I had actually met a mugwump.

Naturally I said I had. Why should only one of us be spewing nonsense?

She asked me if I'd liked it, and if I wanted another taste. She leaned in closer, and smiled, open mouthed.

She flicked her tongue up, and under it I could see a small fleshy thing that writhed like an earthworm trying not to drown. I jerked back without even intending to, and started to believe she was some kind of hallucination or, even worse, a terrible reality. On Sel Souris, you can wind up seeing both.

She laughed then and told me she was teasing, and that I was far too old for that kind of drug. My heart couldn't take it, anymore. I laughed politely, relieved, but my ego still bruised.

She explained that she had been looking for you for a long time and was sure that she could help you discover a great many things. She considered herself to be, in some sense at least, your mother.

I claimed I had long since lost touch, seeing no particular need to foist this madwoman or monster or mugwump upon you. She asked me then if I would mind taking her name and her address, so that if I were to meet you, I might pass it on. I said I would.

She took our picture with a Polaroid Land camera, and that picture is in the box. She also wrote for me, there at the table, a sealed note in an envelope, and gave it to me.

She kissed me on both cheeks and apologized for disturbing me. She left, and I did not see her again. This was weird, as there is only one hotel on Sel Souris that you might want to stay at.

I kept these things, and meant to mail them, but never did. At this point it's likely they'll find the whole package with this letter on top of it after I've finally died, and you'll get it that way.

Getting old is a mortal pain, Adam. If you can avoid it, do.

It occurs to me, in closing, that everything she said may have been true. If so, then I want to tell you on behalf of the whole human race, that we're sorry. We treat everything, but most especially our children, like garbage. We're scared by anything that might sound like hard work, and we resent that you'll go on long after we're in the ground. You seemed every bit as human as most people I know, which is, you know, not so much a compliment as a statement of fact. I'm certain you're terribly lonely. If it makes you feel any better, we all are. We're all creations that our parents abdicated responsibility for. We learned how to act from reading old books, and by spying on happy families through windows. We're all impostors trying to pass as normal people, whatever the hell that even means. You're just a living metaphor for the universal human experience.

If, on the other hand, she was just a terminal fool, and an attention seeker, then pay this no mind.

If she was a Mugwump, drink deep. That's the kind of high men kill and die for.

Your friend,

SOMEONE ELSE'S STORY

William Lee

New York City 1997

178

CHAPTER 13: SEL SOURIS

I stop him there, holding up my hand. "Sel Souris," I say. "Classic. Christ."

"You know of the place?" he asks.

"Yes."

"I am unsurprised. Are you a child of the stars, then, or of the void?"

I shake my head. "I have literally no idea what that even means. All I know is that it keeps coming up over and over in my life. It's a terrible, stupid place and I wish I'd never heard of it."

Frankenstein, or his monster, I suppose, fixes his infantile blue eyes on me and nods.

"I've told you more of my life in the last few minutes than I've told anyone but my

Miranda, who knew most of it anyway. Could you please do me the kindness of explaining what Sel Souris may have to do with you? Your secret is hardly worth preserving in the light of what you and I will soon accomplish here."

"What is that?" I ask. "I'd like to know, frankly."

"I've said already," he says, "Between the two of us, we are going to find a way to give our host immortality. In exchange, will ensure I have what I need for my own artistic endeavours. Once we're done, it's even possible you will go free. It depends, I think, entirely on your level of...commitment."

He smiles again, and I can see he feels he's said something clever. I shrug.

"Fine, Christ," I say, "In the early eighties I was still working as a foreign correspondent. There was no place on Earth I wouldn't fly to, provided it was dangerous enough. I had a death wish, I suppose, or a low threshold for boredom. I don't know. My first real relationship had fallen apart. My fault, with the traveling and the way I held everyone at an arm's length. I think I was half-insane from the world. If you've read *Sodomy in Gomorrah*, you know all of this already."

"I must admit, I haven't. Miranda is looking to acquire a copy for me."

"Anyroad, I made a classic bad decision. I had unprotected sex in Haiti. His name was Jean-Maurice. He meant nothing to me, and in the long run, it turned out that I'd have been just as clever to fire a gun at my own temple. If I had done, I'd have hurt fewer people.

"I had to tell my former lovers about it because I might have been with them once or twice since I'd contracted the disease. Victor had known me the longest, and when I told him he took it very badly. He became obsessed with trying to take care of me, and insisted I try every quack cure that came along. His mania ruined his own relationships, and in the long run, he ran off to Sel Souris because he'd heard there was a man selling a cure to any disease. He'd demanded I go back with him, and when I refused, went back on his own."

Frankenstein shifts his legs forward, and places his elbows on his knees, and his chin on his hands. He looks like a child listening to the teacher.

"It was illegal for British subjects to set foot on the island. They punished him by cutting his tongue out at the root and they removed his eyes before dumping him on a Spanish beach and sailing off again. When he got home, he resisted any attempts at communication, and was eventually put into a hospital. His eyes, I found out, were preserved and on public display on the island.

"It's all a long, mad, story, but it was a year later that I found myself virus free. It wasn't long after that, that I was shot while on assignment in Lebanon. They caught me in the skull. The back of my head came clean off. Six hours later, thankfully without witnesses, I got up and made my way back to the hotel and lied my way out of it.

"My friend Carter, my ex, actually, and Victor's ex too, is sort of magicky. It's nothing you could put your finger on, you know, but he's witchy the way some people are."

Frankenstein nods.

"He thinks that Victor went to Sel Souris fully intending to give his eyes and tongue in blood sacrifice. If I'm still alive, and I'm still young, that's the best answer as to why that I've got. And I'm not the only immortal I know of who can trace their answers to the place. So who knows?"

He lies back down on the couch. "Have you tasted the blood of that island?"

I shrug, "Not that I know of. I'm not sure I even know what you mean."

"How marvelous and strange. Your mysteries are so much more exciting than my answers."

"I'm not very interested in either. Frankly, I'd just like to watch television. Is that so terrible?"

He laughs. "You are the most ridiculous man, you know? You sit before me, a creature of modern myth. You are one of the immortals, objectively greater than any man you may chance to meet. And yet you have no curiosity about the wonders in this world. You are the very model of Christian humility."

"Hardly," I say, "and I looked for answers. I looked for years. Once I realized it would be unrewarding, I stopped. I like liquor. Liquor makes fewer demands than the truth, and it's a hell of a lot easier to get. I suppose I pity you for being such a monster, but I really, honestly just find it hard to give a shit. I just want to put a bullet in your stupid, sadistic, amoral brain, and get back to the bar."

His twisted face seems suddenly sad. "My end is coming. So soon, you hardly need to hasten it, so relax. If it's liquor you want, I'll see you swimming in it. If you want to see me die, then do as I ask of you, and you will. I will surrender hopes that we could have become friends."

"That's probably for the best, yeah?"

Neither of us say anything for a moment. I feel just the slightest bit sorry and then I remember where I am and why.

"What would you have me do?" he asks, standing up, still naked, and he throws a lamp into the wall. The brass clangs against the marble and bends in on itself. "I am what I am, I am what he made me! I cannot help that my soul is every bit as piecemeal as my hateful flesh. I cannot help my whims and my desires! My anger overwhelms me. Yet, even now, do I rend you limb from immortal limb? No. It would do you no evil, but I keep my hand. I channel my rage into art. I teach deeper truths with it. Does this earn me nothing? Will I never be held in the same aspect as a man?"

"I doubt it, mate. It's not your fault. You were made wrong."

He wheels on me and for a second I think he might lower one of those huge fists onto my skull, and it might be better than having to listen to any more. Instead he slams it into the headboard of my bed, and splinters of dark wood fly.

"Damn you!" He rages and stomps about the room, and then falls to his knees on the carpet before me. "How I wish," he says, "that I could tear my own life from its roots and cast it on the floor before you in propitiation. Would that satisfy you?"

"That depends," I say. "What's propitiation mean?"

He takes me by the throat and presses me to the wall just where it meets the ceiling. "You're trying to provoke me! Why would you do that?"

"B...bored," I say.

He releases me, and I drop to the floor. He turns his back and is silent for a long time before he starts back in with his life story some more.

CHAPTER 14: BLOOD OF THE STONE, CHILD OF THE VOID

As promised, the box held the Polaroid of a beautiful black-haired woman, and it also held her sealed letter, which I opened at once.

Dearest Adam, it read, I have looked for you ever since your father's death. I had a strong sense that you were alive, knowing, as I did, the secrets of your creation. It was I, you see, who shared with Victor the secrets of life from death and the transmutation of metals. We were lovers, of a sort, and in a sense I feel maternal toward you.

In another sense, I am more a sister. Like you, my mind persists to flail on in one corpse or another. It has a tenacity that exceeds that of simple flesh. Like you, I exist by regular supplements I take from the so-called human beings that surround me.

I feel you deserve to know the circumstances of your creation. Unlike your father, I feel you are entitled to a mate. If you find me not pleasing, then I will help you in the construction of another. It will not be easy, but it is entirely possible.

You must be lonely. I know that I am. I wish very much to feel again, and I know that you can, with your strength, ensure that I do.

I picked out your first cock myself.

Please contact me at the Hotel Marabou in Cairo. Leave a message, and I will, in time receive it.

I can be patient, for I have waited a long time, and have nothing I own but time. I wonder, can you make a child with me?

Love Always,

Your Miranda.

I did not call. Instead I traveled directly to the Hotel Marabou, and waited there. My days I spent sipping thick strong coffee spiced with cinnamon, and my nights I spent in fevered dreams of her face. I was consumed with her face, and her lewdness and her words, and most especially with her knowledge.

A number of months passed, but time had ceased to have any meaning to me at all.

She arrived in a long black car. A small dark man with curly Semitic hair was with her, and she favoured him with a small kiss as he went inside with her bags. She wore a white linen dress and a hat with a large brim. A scarf hung at her throat, and her sunglasses were large and glamourous. She looked like she had walked out a Fellini film. She strode up the long red carpet to the front door of the hotel, and stood then no further from me that I am from you now. Her head cocked, and she looked in my direction.

I sat in the open patio, also wearing white linen, and white calfskin gloves. Seated, I drew little attention, but she had somehow sensed me. Her eyes met mine, and she lifted her glasses.

She placed one hand on the low black rail of the patio and hopped lightly over it. I stood to meet her, and without a word, she reached her arms up around my neck, and pulled me closer to kiss me. We were in her room a moment later. Her lover, I throttled unto death and cast into the tub in the attached bathroom without saying a word. She did not object.

For a week, we said not two dozen words to each other. Our tongues were too busy at play. She bit and clawed at me like some wild thing, and never ceased to stop fingering my many scars. We did everything two lovers may do to each other. Every kindness and every torture.

The corpse, of course, began to stink.

I crept away for an hour to leave it in the street. When I returned she insisted I bend her over the sink in the room where he'd been. The smell was thick and her moans the louder for it. We were married for the first time a month later.

Eventually, she and I found a need for more in our lives than to simply rut. One night, unbidden, she asked me if it was time to learn of my father.

Much as I hated him, I knew that it was.

We traveled to her home in Spain and spent the time sharing our life stories. There was much for her to tell, and perhaps someday you and she will become friends enough to talk about it. I'd like that. No matter.

My father, my tragic Victor, had met her in Ingolstadt. She had heard the rumours in the scholastic underground of the brilliant young aristocrat engaged in an attempt to bring life to dead flesh through the application of certain chemicals and the galvanic force. She knew this was futile. Flesh is far too subtle to be slapped to alertness through such crude methods. She had lived a hundred years in the world at that time, in six different bodies, and the mechanism by which she had been called forth remained in her possession.

She sought my father out, and he succumbed to her charm. She explained that science was a fine pursuit, but could not accomplish the work of the gods. He claimed that no such force as magic existed. Anything that worked upon the world could be understood in time as something purely natural.

His initial attempts to raise me from the dead through his methods failed, and he agreed to turn to hers. She produced from within her cloak a fragment of stone. Black as fresh soot, but when turned in the light one could see little flecks of deep gold. She said that this was the philosopher's stone, found by Ibrahim Al-Asad in the year 1655. When gently heated, the stone bled a fluid of the same soot-black. This blood had strange properties, among them, the power to transmute death to life. She had seen it raise men from the dead, and she had seen countless doves throttled and returned to life by its administration. She explained that she had no idea how it would work upon such a cobbled together thing such as he had made.

My father took a sample of this fluid; half of it to simply study, and the rest was injected into the femoral artery of his creation upon the slab.

Thus, it came to pass that I was born.

Chapter 15: Blood of the Island, Child of the Stars

Coincidences make me ill. Both of us with these men in our lives who'd granted us eternal life. Both of them dead and gone now, and driven mad before their death. And both named Victor.

The idea of blood drawn from stones is not new either.

In the short period when I was still bothering to look for answers, I met a man named Harry Parker. He was a hundred and thirty years old when I met him, and the Sideshow had pointed me in his direction to see if he had any answers as to my condition. It turned out he didn't. He was one of a group of immortals who could trace their history to the first settlers on Sel Souris. Shortly after their arrival, the island was said to bleed a silver fluid like mercury. Most of the colonists sickened and died. The rest never would. The blood of the island had fused with them and changed them. They could, sometimes, pass immortality on by sharing that fluid, cutting it out from their own bodies.

When I went home to Victor after meeting with Parker, I tried to heal him. I cut my arm, and prayed that silver blood would come forth, land in his mouth and heal him, and change him, and bring him back. Instead, the wound just bled the standard crimson, scabbed over, and went away.

Whatever Harry and his kind are, I am not that.

Neither, it seems to me, are Frankenstein and his bride, but the similarity of their stories does give me pause. And he had asked me about the blood of the island.

Frankenstein stops talking. It's clear he knows I've stopped listening. I wonder if I missed something important. It seems I miss half of everything that matters in my life.

"Have I said something at long last that captures your interest or your pity?" he asks.

"Sort of. You mentioned Al-Asad. That name sent your missus into a screaming fit when I dropped it."

He nods. "I think it's best I show you the Black Stone. My equipment is unloaded now. Get up."

I get up and straighten my clothes. He puts on his robe and leads the way.

The halls of this place are like a hotel. It's a strange and surreal thing to be so far from home, and for the surroundings to be so banal. I mean, of course, every thirty feet or so, there's a painting of the Beloved Leader smiling down at me, but aside from that, it's a lot like any other fucking hotel.

"The original stone had gone missing," he says, "long before I met her. And the fragment she possessed stopped giving forth blood, and turned to a kind of dust. She'd kept the dust in an envelope, and then, on a whim, renounced sentimentality, and tossed it away with her last host. The name Al-Asad was all that we had to track its origins by. I spent large sums to track down any work of an alchemist by the name Al-Asad. Eventually a dealer in occult paraphernalia contacted me.

"He had in his possession, a scroll, still in Arabic, written by Al-Asad. Also, with the scroll, were writings about Al-Asad, compiled by various hands. Aleister Crowley had brought the package to England, then traded it away in payment of a debt. Since then it had mouldered in a basement."

We get into a black limousine, and he says something to the driver in Korean before continuing. I am looking out the window and realize this is all a large military base. There are images of that bespectacled little toad everywhere. It makes me a little dizzy. The driver's eyes flit nervously from the road to the rear-view mirror to look at us.

"Al-Asad," he says, "was never well known, but was often mentioned in passing in books of occult history as something of a crackpot and, in your terms, an apocalyptic. There was no sign that he had ever found any real power or success. I knew differently, or at least Miranda's acquaintance had been told he had.

"I had learned some Arabic in the Foreign Legion, but the scroll itself was so damaged by water and simple age that I could make out nearly nothing. The handwritten papers attached, on the other hand alleged themselves to be a translation of this fragment."

Chapter 16: A Sun, Blackened

The greater part of the sun was covered in an uneven blackness that looked more like the mouth of Shaitan than that of the Earth, nor did our astrologers expect such an interaction of the spheres. No man watching could think this a demonstration of the powers of Allah. The stones at our feet began to howl in sympathy or in fear, and some small number of them did burst like bubbles, scattering their remains onto the sand.

I was not alone among those witnesses who then heard a voice which spoke not out loud but rather seemed to swell inside our head and stick like pitch. It spoke not in words but in hungers. My brother did fall to the ground and begin to scratch behind his ear with his own foot like some flea-bitten dog. The eyes of my third wife did begin to bleed, and also there came from my own hand a growth that felt like stone.

The voice was not Shaitan, nor did it claim to be. It was the voice of the outermost dark where the dead were gathered as fuel to terrible engines. The void which spoke seemed as one with all there was, and I could not comprehend a hundredth part of what it whispered.

I saw a great sailing ship blown by the rotten breath of the damned and crewed by things without shape or flesh. These ghuls and afrits and evil djinni craved flesh and found our smell pleasing.

The stone now falling was both anchor and lighthouse, and the ship of fleshly lust and hungry death was coming as surely as day followed unto day. We were to enjoy its bounty and grow fat and luscious and toothsome. In four hundred years the outer dark would snuff out our campfires and all flesh would be raped. All flesh would then end.

My hands had turned to stone, and ichor did drip from them onto the sand. Where it landed, the ground itself did writhe with twisted vitality.

The sun did then likewise return to blessed life, and the voice did recede.

I bid my son to draw his sword and strike my hand from my wrist, and when he refused, I bid my wife likewise, and she did as I had asked.

My wrist was then thrust against the heated edge of a sword. My own wits deserted me, and my last hearing was the sound of jackals laughing.

The stone that had once been my hand whispered terrible secrets to my youngest son.

In the dead of the night, did he make off with it, and went about the dark business of sorcery, falling to temptation. It is said that he calls forth demons to take up flesh and do his bidding, and these demons are at first terrified and grieving, and then filled with praise for him. They will do whatever he asks, terrified that he might cast them back to the terrible dark place from whence they came.

I feel that they speak with deceit, instead walking the earth only to inspect the cattle before slaughter.

The ship of butchers and of lechers will come, if Allah wills it, and there is nothing any man may do. I can only live in the hopes that Allah the merciful would not doom my many-times grandchildren to such a fate. There must be some stone he cast down to balance the great dark.

If there is the outer dark, perhaps the inner light is also.

I cannot sit idly while my son courts such power. My brothers and I will follow him, and I will try to speak reason to him. If I cannot, then I will see the stone cast to the sea, and I will pray he can atone to Allah in the moments until he....

Chapter 17: A Sudden Commotion

That's all there was to that fragment," he says, "and I may have misspoken some of it. My memory is strong but not so strong as once it was. There were others, and in time they led me to the Black Stone itself."

"So she thought I was some kind of sorcerer?" I interrupt, half smiling. "Don't I bloody wish? Where are we going?"

He points out the window to the quonset less than a hundred yards from us.

"My new studio," he says. "I am given everything I could need, indefinitely. Of course, by my calculations, we're not more than twenty years until the end of flesh. I'm willing to gamble that I can keep appealing to his whimsy that long. Especially if I am successful."

The car stops and he gestures for me to get out.

I smell the contents of the building the moment the wind shifts, and my saliva goes over all metallic. He keeps walking, and I stay where I am. He turns his head over his shoulder to look at me. It's worse than the smell of death and rot. Something in that building will overwhelm my mind if I draw a single step closer. For all my bluster and insolence and my façade of cool, I am more scared than I have ever been. My own body has drawn a line here that it will not let me cross.

There are guards posted at the door to the quonset, and others at a slight remove with guns at the ready. The sun is bright, but it is not especially hot. The guards all look pale, and sweaty and shaky. They have spent more time next to this building and whatever horror it contains, and they are not at all well.

"Come," he says, and it's a command, the way one speaks to a dog, and one of the guards startles at the urgency of his tone

"Fuck you. Keep me as your bloody prisoner, bore me with your story of woe, use me as a guinea pig in your little experiments, but I will not look at your art anymore. You're shite at it."

He snarls like an animal and picks me up in both hands squeezing hard. I fight back, kicking at his belly and balls with both feet. He grunts, but I might as well be kicking a brick wall for all of the good that it does me. His sneer widens, his cleft lip pulling back to show his huge square teeth, and he does something to me that I can't believe.

Still gripping me, he tears me completely in half lengthwise and throws me to the ground.

I see my left arm and leg, one of my lungs, and most of my guts lying in the grass a few feet away. I feel no pain at all. It's possible my own body is too shocked to react.

He snarls in Korean, and the soldiers hesitate for just a second, and one of them, in panic, raises his gun vaguely at Frankenstein. It's enough to send him over the edge of his mad rage. He grabs the soldier and swings him by the leg at two more, who have drawn nearer, knocking them like ninepins. The rest of the soldiers begin to fire, and his flesh erupts. He is rocked back, jerking slightly at each impact. He falls to his knees and then forward on his face.

Assault rifles are nothing to fuck with. I can hear him moaning, but he is not getting up.

The doors to the quonset slam open. A thick smell of death and fermentation come as well. Miranda almost flies from the door, hands outstretched and clawing at anything in reach. Her scream breaks the windows of the limousine, and the soldiers clamp their hands over their ears. She moves with a speed that reminds me of falling and stands over me.

Her dark hair rings her face, and her eyes glow with hate. There is no wind, but her hair moves, seeming to twitch with rage.

"You did this," she says, "I knew you for him the moment I saw you! You mean to cast me back, and to deny my beloved his only wish! You're not half the man your son was. You don't have his dreams or his mercy."

I want to say something, or at least run away, but I really, literally am not half the man I used to be, and she is off her nut, shrieking and spitting mad. The best course I have is to lie here and bleed.

She seizes me in her hands, sinking her forearm into my well-open chest cavity, and she pulls out my heart. I feel it come free. She starts to eat it in front of me while I watch, dropping me back to the dirt. She does not see the single soldier coming up behind. He drives his fixed bayonet up under the soft spot at the base of her skull, and into her brain and shudders in wide-eyed horror.

She dies instantly, dropping like so much timber. Her face lands up next to me, her mouth open, and I see her tongue moving. Under it, something is crawling to be free. It is soot black, with golden eyes. It has no face at all, but it is hungry. I feel it raging in my head, and it inches forward for my face. It lands on the sand and keeps crawling closer.

I open my mouth to scream, but no air is pushed through my voice box. I have no lungs at the moment. I try to hurl myself back, but my remaining leg is dead to me, spine in two pieces. The little control I have of my good arm is only enough to slap the sand aimlessly on the other side of my body from her.

The soldier who killed her sees that I am alive, and I'm sure he has seen men live for a time when blown in half, but never with such vigor. He has never seen such a thing as this worm. He is frozen into inactivity for several seconds, and just as I think the black and golden thing will take me, he brings down his rifle onto it. It bleeds its black blood into the dirt. I feel it die. The voices in my head cry out and then fade away.

Frankenstein screams and rises. I try to warn the brave, terrified man who has saved me twice, but all he sees in my eyes is blind panic, and not for long. Frankenstein throws him aside and stands over his bride, his eyes wide with grief. More soldiers have arrived and are pointing guns at him. An officer is shouting commands, but he doesn't hear them.

He falls to his knees, shoving me roughly aside and digging through the grass for the little bug from inside of her, and he finds it. His voice rings louder than any human voice as he howls in pain. He grabs his own chest and pulls free a great clump of flesh, which he tosses to the ground. Flesh is just a garment to him, and he's rending his. The soldiers lower their guns, confused.

Frankenstein covers his face with his hands, sobbing. That and the soft wind are the only sounds. Soldiers in hazmat gear come to close the quonset door. I am grateful for such small favours.

When the soldiers come closer to inspect me, Frankenstein turns and snarls at them. They back off.

After what seems like half an hour, he gets to his feet and runs. His stride is long, if ungraceful, and he is soon gone. Nobody pursues him. The soldiers check their fallen comrade, and I wish that I could speak, and I wish that I had picked up any Korean at all when I was here twenty years ago or so. No such luck.

My flesh itches as it regrown, and they stare at me goggle-eyed. I gesture awkwardly at the other part of me, and one of them, god love him, brings it to me. He tries to scoop my insides inside, and press the parts together. One or two of the others help, and I vow never to speak ill of the minions of tyranny again. It's much faster to re-knit myself together than it is to re-grow. In a few minutes, I have both the breath and the agony to scream.

A medic gives me some kind of drug and I pass out gratefully.

Chapter 18: Anticlimax

It's the dead of night, and I am in a hospital bed. There are wires all over me. A soldier with a gun leans against one wall, half asleep. I feel fine. I probably am fine, aside from being in North Korea.

I sit up, and the soldier startles.

"It's okay," I say in English, "hoping my tone is calming." I smile, and that's not very hard to do right after discovering I actually can move. I keep my hands where he can see them.

"Thank fucking hell you're awake," the soldier says, in a posh accent.

"Cath," I say. It's a statement, not a question.

"Yeah," she says. "This is a fine situation you find yourself in, isn't it?"

"Yes," I answer. "It is, thanks. Any idea what's going on?"

"Well, the North Korean military is on stand-by and looking for a seven-foot-tall man accused of going berserk and murdering several soldiers. Also, Jong-Il has been making all manner of crazy speeches about how the power of North Korea is unquestioned and unchallenged, and that his rule will last a thousand years. So nothing actually out of the ordinary."

I laugh and reach for a packet of cigarettes that isn't there, and hasn't been for years. "Seriously. Cath, what now?"

"Eager to be my friend now, aren't you?"

"Yes! I bloody am. I'll fucking go down on you in that soldier's body, if it will get me the hell out of this country."

"Spare me," she says, and lets loose a sigh.

"Cath, please."

She takes a few steps closer to the bed. "Fine, you squalling infant. Here's the deal. There is a boat docked in town here. It's a freighter that will be leaving for Japan in the morning. The Sideshow has arranged for you to be taken aboard, hidden and sent back to England from Tokyo. In return, you are going to come to the offices, and you are going to debrief us on every damned thing that's happened here. All of it. For as long as we like, until we say it's okay."

"That is fine with me, Christ. I'm in. Sign me up. If it gets me out of this mad business, I'll do it."

"Good. I think this should go smoothly...."

"Cath," I say, "Do you know what's in the quonset?"

"No, but the satellite imagery shows us that it's been shelled."

"Shelled?"

"Shelled."

"I am so fucking glad I didn't go in there."

"Well, you would be, wouldn't you? That was our best chance at finding out exactly what the hell that freak was up to."

"Which, of course, was your whole reason for getting me involved, wasn't it? For making me bring up Al-Asad."

She shrugs and I remember that I hate her.

"I don't give a slippery shit about what he was up to," I say. "I just want to go home. Every time I get involved with anything you call interesting it always turns tits up."

Cath looks out the window, and then flashes her torch out the window at someone twice. "It's time. Can you walk?"

I think of Lisa and the kid taking tickets at the Metro, and nod.

"I'll bloody well walk out of here," I say, quoting my least favorite film.

She nods, and we go out the door, down the hall, and quickly into a very plain black car and to the docks. I don't know how the Sideshow distracted so many of the guards, and in my own true fashion, happily I don't care.

As I get aboard the ship, the Japanese captain and his first mate keep bowing at me like I'm someone important. I thank them politely and return the bow. Cath tells me to hurry up. I spare one last look at North Korea, and duck below.

I'll no' forget ye' Kim Jong-Il, I think perversely. I try not to think of what sort of punishment Cath's host is going to suffer for letting me get away. I owed the anonymous soldiers of North Korea a debt I had no way to repay.

I am bundled in a smuggler's compartment behind some shipping containers. A sense of avoided deja vu is strong. There is a cot inside, a small chemical toilet, ready to eat meals in foil packages and about 40 fucking beautiful plastic bottles of water. I settle in for the duration.

I have no idea in the world what I'd walked into the middle of, nor what I'd escaped from. As usual.

EPILOGUE

Ten days later I am on the streets of London, free of obligation. My former co-workers are not pleased with me, but I have, in fact, told them everything I know. Like the police they are, it's not quite enough. It doesn't quite tell the story. I missed out on most of the important parts. Of course, this is my basic problem, isn't it? I'm the supporting character. I have this tendency to keep ending up in the middle of someone else's story. Is it any wonder that I've given up caring about the mysteries?

From a pay phone in London, I call my flat in Canada, and get my messages. This is a casual feat of technology that still stuns me more than any ancient scroll. I skip through the sixteen police calls, and the five frantic calls from Heather, and then there is one that gets my attention.

"Tom," says a voice from my distant past, low and soft, "This girl of yours has some serious issues with her self-esteem, and it needs looking into. Not the least of her problems is that she seems to think she's your daughter or something, while, in fact, she's much more interesting than you ever were. It's Carter, by the way," he adds, as though I could ever forget the sound of his voice, "Lisa's come to stay with us...."

There is a sound of a slight struggle, and I hear Lisa say "Hi TOM!", as though she is having the time of her life, a kind of ten-year old glee in her voice, before Carter wrestles the phone back.

"Never mind," he says, "She's probably yours, Christ." That last sentence he growls in imitation of me, and I touch the front of the phone box tenderly as though it was his cheek. "Please call us, won't you? She's nearly unbearable."

I am about to hang up the phone when the machine reminds me there is another message. "Hello, Tom," Frankenstein says. "I wanted you to know…"

I terminate and erase the message. I'd just as soon not know.

Twenty-five minutes later, I am in front of the building where Carter and his husband now live.

I press the buzzer, and they let me up. Carter answers the door, and looks at me with his dark still eyes, now set a little deeper in a nest of fine smile lines. He smiles with the ease of a child and I put my hand on his cheek.

"Hullo," I say.

"Hiya."

He is viciously elbowed aside by a ruffian with too many lip piercings. She practically jumps into my arms as she wraps her arms around me. She doesn't even say hello.

"Thank you," says Niles, stepping into view, "for sending us your gothic troublemaker."

I just smile and shrug.

Carter clears his throat and shoves Lisa with both hands, very deliberately, to get her out of the way.

"As I was saying," he says, "Hiya."

I kiss him, and then I kiss his husband, who more or less pretends not to like it, or me, at all.

A few hours later, after a late meal, Carter and Niles head to bed. It seems a little early to me, and to Lisa. Neither of them is particularly young anymore. That makes me a little sad, and makes me feel a little guilty. It also makes me love them both that little bit more. If it were me, and I were fifty years old, and my old mate was still practically a kid, I think I'd resent them. They didn't seem to mind a bit, or at least never gave me the slightest indication they would.

It's clear that the bedroom door stands open as an invitation, and I admit to considering it.

Lisa sits on the couch with her legs curled up under her. I am sitting Indian style on the floor and she hands me a cup of tea.

"This isn't Dublin," I say. "You do know that, right?"

"Yeah," she says. "I was scared and I didn't have anyone I could talk to, you know. Then I remembered all the things you said about Carter and Niles in *Sodomy in Gomorrah*, and I could tell how safe you'd felt here and I realized that they were like family to you, and sort of...well, I found your address book and...."

"I'll hear about this until I'm an old man, you know."

"So what now?" she asks.

"We can't go home. Frankenstein probably means to track us down and rip you to shreds in front of me, or some crazy nonsense like that. Furthermore, I think it's time that I faked my death or something and started over. I think Tom Bradstreet has too much baggage at this point."

"You know how to do that? Just fake your death?"

"No, but I firmly believe that we'll figure it out."

"What about me?"

"I think we'll have to put an end to you as well. Happily, I'll probably make a new friend immediately who is very like you in most ways."

"I should probably be pissed off about this, shouldn't I?" she asks, putting a finger on her chin, posing in thought.

"If I were you, I'd be murderous about it." I say.

"Oddly enough, I don't give a shit."

"I'm glad."

"Me too."

"Do you want to talk about what happened to me the last few weeks," I ask. "You have a perfect right, all things considered."

"Maybe some time," she says, "but not right now. I'm just really happy to see you."

"You've got good instincts. This was a wonderful place to flee to. The past always is."

She smiles and leans back, blowing across the surface of her tea. I imagine this is of higher importance to her than for normal people, as she has an induction coil grafted to her upper lip.

"Do you want to go see a movie?" she asks.

"Oh god," I say, tears coming to my eyes, though I've no idea why, "very much."

Niles has a Polaroid he used to use back in the days when he was a detective and therefore very slightly interesting. I use it to snap a shot of Lisa and I smiling broadly.

On the bottom, I write in felt marker, *We belong dead! Call you from the afterlife, once we're settled in. Much love, and thanks.*

We scrawl our names. She kisses the picture leaving a dark purple lip-print, and we head into the night.

ABOUT THE AUTHOR

Laird Ryan States was born in 1971, in Calgary Alberta. He spent his childhood and early adult life in Saskatoon, Saskatchewan, which is an excellent place to grow up for a writer, as it's at least as weird as Austin, Texas. He currently lives in a lovely old house in Edmonton Alberta, with his best friend, novelist Gayleen Froese, three dogs, and so many reptiles and invertebrates that he has lost count.

Someone Else's Story is his third book, and a sequel to his self-published *Silver Bullets* and *Sleeping Underwater*, which is kindly published by The Seventh Terrace. It is part of a cycle of stories and mixed media art about the island of Sel Souris. He has nearly completed the sequel to this book, tentatively titled *Wonderland*, and is many hundreds of thousands of words into a long novel about pro-wrestling and the end of the world that also has loose ties to this cycle.

Ryan has loved Frankenstein's monster since he was a small child, and though he thoroughly takes the piss out of him in this work, honestly believes him to be one of the greatest creations in literature, and feels a kinship with him that is occasionally uncomfortable.

The Seventh Terrace

Also Available from The Seventh Terrace

30 to 50 Feral Hogs

Hell Hath No Sorrow like a Woman Haunted

Unfortunate Elements of My Anatomy

Terrace V – Penitent's Gold

Terrace VI – Forbidden Fruit

Terrace VII – Wall of Fire

Trace & Solomon: Torrington

Sleeping Underwater

The Black City Beneath

End of the Loop

Futility: Orange Planet Horror

Infractus

Suicide Stitch

Fishing with the Devil